The Floating World - Urban Erotica

A.A.Cain

Published by: A.A.Cain,

PO Box 117, Campbelltown, South Australia, 5074.

Email: writingbyaacain.gmail.com

First Edition: 2019

ISBN:

epub   978-0-9876330-3-3

print   978-0-9876330-5-7

Printed and distributed by Lulu.com

Contents

Epigraph   3

Amanda in the City   5
   The Cambridge Street Café   7
   On Another Corner   13
   Amanda at the Counter   15
   On the Train   19
   The Art Gallery   27
   In the Hotel Room   41
   The Blue Silk Dress   59
   At the Private Function   69
   In an Upstairs Room   75

Gabriela - Twelve Silken Buttons   93
   Closing Day   95
   In Gabriela's Room   101
   The First Day Back   111
   In the Garden   115
   A Black Velvet Choker   123
   The Last Button   135

About the Author   153

Readers' Comments   155

Epigraph

During the Tokugawa Period in Japan (1600-1868) the word *ukiyo* came to describe the meaningless pleasure and ennui that was the lifestyle for many people in the cities, particularly Edo, Kyoto, and Osaka. "Floating World" is the English translation.

It is said that the geisha, or courtesan, occupied a separate reality known as *karyukai,* or the "flower and willow world". The geisha entertained their customers with the tea ceremony, and with a cultured presentation of music, dance, and conversation.

Amanda in the City

The Cambridge Street Café

It was Adam's first day in a new office, a five block walk from the bus stop. He knew he couldn't function without a morning cup of coffee, but this end of town was new to him, not familiar at all. So he checked out both sides of the street as he walked along, looking for a typical city block café, hoping that the barista would be good, and the distance from the office just right.

Was this the best there was? The Cambridge Street Café? An unimaginative but honest trading name. Christ, red chequered table cloths and sepia photographs of Paris. Fucking Monday and he's cynical already, the café is a cliché. A bell jangled when he pushed the door open, but the counter was deserted.

"Sorry, I was out back in the kitchen, what will you have?"

You, he thought, caught instantly by her grace and shy smile.

"A medium latte, take away, please."

"OK, my pleasure," she replied, turning to the espresso machine; her hands busy, her long hair twisting outwards with the turn of her body.

No, mine, Adam thought, as he watched her precise movements, her slim fingers reaching for a paper cup then gripping the tamper, pressing down the coffee, flicking the tap. As the steam rushed into the milk, her hands became still as she held the stainless steel jug, both hands around its body, judging the temperature. Perfection. The woman became a moment in time in front of him, and Adam gazed upon her. The second hand on the wall clock froze, tick but no tock. The ceremony had begun.

Adam watched the woman as she concentrated on serving him, her hands slow, her eyes ever so slightly narrowed in a small frown and her lips ever so slightly parted. She was slender, narrow hipped with a slim waist, her breasts barely shaping the front of her waitress' tunic. Her hair was long, coiled black falling down her back, falling to the line of her hips. Adam imagined that silken black hair wrapping over his arm, if he could take her by the waist and escort her to a dance floor.

Feeling herself observed, the woman turned to her customer. "I have not seen you here before, have I?"

Her accent was foreign; Hong Kong Chinese, Adam thought, English not her native language.

"No. Today is my first day in a new job. I'm going to the headquarters building a block down."

"Oh yes, I know it."

She snapped a plastic lid onto the paper cup.

"There. Coffee for you." Her words had a slight upwards lilt, as if the statement was also a question.

Adam passed her the right money, touching her fingers as he did so. Her fingers were warm. The woman smiled at his touch. That was an answer.

"Thank you." Adam's voice softened, and he too smiled.

The door jangled behind him as he went out to the street. The decor of the café didn't matter, thought Adam, the woman was a lovely start to his day, a delicacy. Her coffee was good, too.

The next day was the same, Adam's gaze, her quiet serenity. This time he picked up a loyalty card, which she stamped with a smiley face in one little box. Her words were the same:"There, coffee for you," with an upwards lilt in her voice.

Adam gave her a bank note, and she brushed his fingers with hers as she gave back the change. Her fingers were warm. The coffee was hot.

The day after that it was raining. She smiled as Adam entered the café and shook out his umbrella by the door, and she turned immediately to the espresso machine to prepare his order. This time he gave her the right money, and their little touch in the morning was a simple human contact between a man and a woman. It was only a small thing, but became everything in the moment between the tick of the clock and the tock.

Over the days their ritual was the same, and it became a small ceremony between them. They were both formal with it, and the sun slowly shifted its light on the stone tiled floor as the season lengthened and a little friendship was made in the mornings. The shadow of a decorative branch by the door marked the passage of time. Some days the shadow was dark and etched on the floor, the sun bright outside; other days the shadow was gone, and it rained.

Over the weeks, Adam told her of his children who he loved; and she told him of her mother in Shanghai who was old, and she worried. Out back in the kitchen, her husband would look through the serving hatch and nod his greeting. Adam wondered what the quiet cook thought of this man who looked upon his wife with affection, whose fingers always traced hers as his money was given.

It was a subtle, lingering movement. Adam's palm would be turned up, the coins resting in the cup of his fingers. She would lightly slide her fingers over the top of his, covering the coin in the shadow of her hand, and their hands would turn together so that her palm received his offering. Adam would slide his fingers from hers, his payment made. "Coffee for you," she would say, but they both knew the payment wasn't for the coffee.

Even on the tenth days, when there was no money between them (the little smiley faced stamp keeping its record of the passing days), she would return the card to Adam's palm, her fingers long and fine against his, caressed and slow.

At first, their hands would only lightly touch, eyes looking down at the movement of their fingers, but over the days they learned each other's touch and they looked up to each other's face. Adam saw her pupils go wide and dark with his caress, and she controlled the intake of her breath. After she shut the cash drawer of the till, her fingers would go each day to the same place on her throat to feel the heat of her rising flush. Adam felt his own deeper pulse, and her lips reddened. But their fingers never held, only lingered.

After many days, Adam told her that his time in the building down the block was ending, he was going somewhere else. She in turn explained that she and her husband were selling the café and returning to China, for her mother was ill. So the little love between their fingers would be parted, and their hearts would beat a little slower.

On the afternoon of Adam's last Friday, he went into the café just before it closed for the day. "Hello, I've come to say goodbye. It's my last day today, so I thought I would drop by to see you, before I go."

"Oh, that is sad. But we close next week anyway, and we'll be gone, too."

Her husband came from the kitchen out back and stood, waiting. She came from behind the counter and surprised Adam, coming right up to embrace him, holding him tight. She was slender and fragile in his arms, and Adam held her. She laid her cheek on his shoulder and he held her close. He looked up, and saw her husband looking at him. The man nodded a greeting, to acknowledge this man in his woman's quiet mornings.

Adam kissed her hair and her hand pressed back against his arm, this first time held for them both to remember. As they parted, he ran his fingers down the long length of her hair to the top of her hip, and pressed his hand there, where her hair ended. If they had danced, he would have pulled her body close to his, his hand sliding from her hip to her small waist. But they weren't dancing, only their fingers had danced.

Adam left the delicate woman and turned to her husband, offering his hand in a last greeting and a thanks. They shook hands, strangers in a café, men bonded because of a woman.

Adam turned back to the woman and touched his fingers to her cheek. He mouthed the word, goodbye. Her fingers touched his lips, and the clock stopped.

"There. No more coffee for you." Her voice was soft and low, her eyes bright.

"No, no more coffee for me. Thank you for all of them, they were just right. Lovely."

You're lovely, Adam thought, standing there in your purple waitress' uniform, your long hair falling, twisting. Longing for her, he turned and went out the door, turning left down the footpath. A rich, slightly acrid scent of her lingered in his senses.

It wasn't until he was on the bus that Adam realised why the pungency of her scent was so familiar. It was on her fingers, a last payment for him, the hem of her dress lifted and her fingers dipped. So quickly, while Adam was shaking her husband's hand.

On Another Corner

With his new job Adam found another café, this one on a corner facing east, the morning sun hot as the days grew longer. His order was always the same, a latte. It gave him familiarity and constancy, the small ceremony a meditation, stopping the world for a moment. Adam sometimes wondered if life was just a collection of moments, with living the long spaces in between.

This girl's movements were slow and unrushed. There was rarely a queue in the corner café, and the barista filled the space with her own time. Adam would sit, and his long gaze went behind the counter. The girl was curvier than the Chinese woman, and younger. Adam didn't mind her youth nor her curves, both were delectable.

She kept the milk in a fridge behind the counter, and would bend at the waist to reach for it; her thighs tight and her ass nicely rounded in black jeans, the crisp rectangle of a phone in her back pocket. The girl was Arabic, and Adam imagined a curling thickness of black hair along her lips as she bent. She pulled hair back from her face, and a fine down of blackness was there too, on the nape of her neck.

Her darkness reminded Adam of a girl at school, whose forearms were also soft with dark shadow. He looked around, but the ghost had gone.

This girl didn't touch, and Adam didn't dare. She did place a gold wrapped chocolate on the top of the plastic cover of his cup each day, and after two weeks, she gave him two chocolates. She was a silent girl hardly saying a word, but the second chocolate gave Adam a simple thrill. He was a favoured customer and it was her quiet wordless offering.

Her silence was a serenity, her slow pace a contemplation, and the room was always still. A fly buzzed. Adam wondered if the monks of Skellig Michael had ever drunk coffee. If this girl had been there amongst the stones they surely would have, to hear her silence.

Her darkness would have been another meditation, Adam thought. Coffee wouldn't have been necessary with this girl, if her darkness was what mattered. She glanced across at him. Her darkness mattered. Adam closed his eyes to keep her glance deep in his mind.

The real delight though, and the reason Adam kept coming back to this corner of the block (for her coffee wasn't so good) was the simple movement the girl made when she reached up for a cup from a high shelf.

After she got the milk from the fridge, that movement with its promise of a dark place, and set the milk to hcat, the girl would reach high to get a cup. Each time she did so, a small triangle of flesh would show, just above her hip.

They say the most beautiful part of a geisha is the back of her neck, and that is why there's no make-up there. Adam knew that was wrong – this girl's triangle of skin, dark and brief and just above her hip, was her most beautiful place, her flat belly a promise beyond.

She glanced across at Adam, and saw the line of his gaze. She reached a little higher.

Amanda at the Counter

"Good morning, will you have your usual?"

The coffee girl was slender, slight. A curved line of mascara extended her almond shaped eyes, giving her a touch of the middle-east, of Egypt. Three diamond ear studs lay on the inside of each ear, and she wore a small gold ring on the top of each lobe. Delicate jewellery, complimenting her elfin face, dusky skinned, dark eyed.

"Wait, don't tell me, let's see if I can remember." Her voice had a slight huskiness to it. Adam listened, his attention captured. "Black coff... no, wait, latte, that's right, isn't it?"

Adam smiled at her, liking the way she wanted to remember him, his order, and to be a part of his morning. "Yes, that's right, a latte, take away." He gave her the right money. Her hand was slim and small.

She looked up at him. "Your name, wait, let me see if I can... Adr... no, Adam. You're Adam."

"Yes, I'm Adam," he replied, liking her more for remembering his name, out of the hundreds of customers who visited the café.

"I'll remember your name now, it begins with an A, same as mine." The girl rang up the sale, and passed a ticket down the counter to the barista.

"Anna?" he wondered. "You look like you could be an Anna."

"Do I? No, I'm an Amanda."

"Oh, I was hoping I could guess your name, these next few days. Hello Amanda, it's nice to meet you."

"You too, Adam."

Their formality was a friendly thing, and so they were introduced. As he stood waiting for his coffee, Adam admired the girl. He liked small, graceful women, and this girl was young and slim. A student, maybe, paying her way through uni. Or perhaps a graduate, he couldn't really tell her age. Somewhere between twenty and twenty-three or four, he guessed. Young enough to be his daughter, anyway.

The barista poured Adam's order, and called his name. Adam took the coffee, took two sips to lower the level before it spilled, and went out into the street. As he turned left up the footpath, he glanced inside and saw Amanda serving a line of customers. Her long hair, tied up in a high pony tail, swung behind her head as she turned to the cash register.

Over the days and weeks that followed, Amanda would ask Adam on the Mondays how his weekend was. He told her about mending the blown down fence, and one morning she ex- plained her black painted fingernails for a party the previous Friday night. He discovered then that Antony was her boyfriend, "Ant wore black too, he never does."

Usually, Amanda's nails were a light red, or a pink, cut short, but it was a Goth party, so this time she was all in black. Her fingers were fine and slender, no rings worn. She was feminine and young.

Come the colder winter mornings, Adam asked Amanda what time she got up, to always be at work when the café opened. "I set my alarm for a quarter to five," she replied. Adam's heart ached for this waif of a girl getting up in the dark, to make men and women coffee in the morning.

"That's not right, is it? It must be so cold that time of the morning. I'm still fast asleep." He smiled at her, his fondness for her in his voice. "You poor thing."

She laughed. "Yes, the house is freezing. My shower is always longer than it should be, to warm me up."

Adam looked at the girl with her dark eyes, imagining her arching her neck under the shower head, falling water heating her skin, her fingers caressing the shampoo from her long hair. With her arms stretched above her head, her breasts would be small, tight on her frame. She was slim and small, and her hair was long.

He thought her skin would be smooth and warm, and if he could inhale her scent, musky and spiced. He wanted to hold a big towel around her so she wouldn't be cold when she stepped from the shower. His little coffee girl and the mornings so cold.

Amanda wasn't just his coffee girl in the mornings. One lunchtime, Adam came back from the laksa house where he had eaten, and bought a coffee to sit. Another waitress took the order, but Amanda brought it out to him, a big smile on her face. "I didn't know you came here for lunch," she said. "How are you?"

"I usually don't, Adam replied, "but this sun is lovely and warm. It's nice to sit and read the paper, soak up some heat."

"Yes, it is, isn't it?" She touched him lightly on the arm. "Enjoy your coffee."

"I will honey, thanks." Adam's endearment was automatic, a fondness, triggered by her touch. Amanda was a girl his daughter's age after all, and he was affectionate with his daughter, too. She smiled at his words, her eyes smiled.

Adam touched the cup where Amanda's fingers had been. She really was a honey. He watched her as she walked away, and there was a sexy swing to her plain black waitress' skirt, even in her practical shoes. Her calves were taut, firmly muscled. She was on her feet all day, and was fit. Adam smiled. Amanda was a sweet thing, as she walked from him, her ponytail swinging high on her head. Adam imagined her hair falling long down her back, and pushing it back from her cheek with his finger.

Others did too. Another day Adam shifted his chair aside so that a woman in a wheelchair could get to the adjacent table, her glittering rings and jewellery catching the sun and her deep cleavage shadowed. Like Amanda she had Cleopatra eyes, but her lips were deep and red. Heat radiated from her like smoke. Damn, she's sexy, thought Adam, distracted.

Adam had been served already and was shuffling pages of his newspaper when the woman's partner arrived. Her man was slim and blond, touching her shoulder as he sat beside her. Adam glanced across, his eye caught by the movement. He smiled at their affection, it was obvious in the way they leaned in towards each other, their heads close. Adam realised the woman was pregnant, her belly a full delight as she sat in the wheelchair. No wonder she was oozing sex, he thought, she must be a cocktail of swirling hormones.

He looked up a moment later to see Amanda bring the couple their coffee and a glass of water, all on a tray. Adam didn't catch what the woman said to the girl, but did see Amanda's spontaneous smile in response. The girl glowed, sometimes. As she walked away, and of course his eyes followed, he heard the woman say, "She's pretty."

Adam's attention was caught by the words, and even more so by her partner's response. "Yes, she is. Would you like her?"

So it's not just me, then, thought Adam, intrigued by the couple's conversation. He watched out of the corner of his eye, his ears pricked for her response. There was a short pause, then the woman tapped her fingers to her lips, twice. "Yes, she'd be nice and tender, I think."

Wow, thought Adam, Amanda makes quite an impression, not just on me. The way the woman described Amanda as a morsel, a sweet taste of something to be eaten, intrigued Adam. He had imagined the girl's skin soft under the touch of his fingers, but he'd not thought of the taste of her before now. He pondered the idea of the girl on the tip of his tongue. He imagined her lips would have a light musky scent, a little exotic, a little spicy. They would part softly under his finger tips, and she would sigh at his delicate touch.

He finished his coffee and pushed the cup away from him, his fingers touching the place where Amanda's fingers had been. He wondered where else her fingers would go.

On the Train

Amanda sat back in her usual seat in the rail carriage, her eyes closed against the flickering shadows from trees alongside the track. The clicker clack of the wheels on the track was hypnotic, and the occasional bump as the train lurched through points bounced her bag on her lap.

She used the brisk walk to the station to clear her head from the shift and swell of people through the café door each day, like the tide on a beach with its surge and drop. The half hour on the train, forty-five minutes if it was slow, was her stop time, her shift from work to play. But God, she was always so tired at the end of the day, so she didn't get time to play. Or sing or dance, like she used to. She tried, but her time was like a cat's, sleeping to get energy back for the next day.

What had Adam said, his deep blue eyes smiling down at her when she told him of her alarm clock time? Oh, you poor thing, that's too early isn't it? I'm still warm in my bed at that time. Amanda shifted in her seat, her fingers gripping the side of her bag, an unconscious push of it to the base of her belly. The train rocked, and her thighs clenched to keep her body from swaying. I'm still warm in my bed.

Amanda liked Adam's friendly face looking at her, his blue eyes steady, his smile creased at the corners of his eyes. She always tried to remember her regular customers' names. His was easy, and she remembered on the third day. A for Adam, the same initial as her own name. He thought she looked like an Anna. She wondered who his Anna was, this girl she was like. Amanda drifted, her mind lulled. He called me honey.

She shifted in her seat, and remembered the tall, slim man at lunchtime, lost in his own world as he gazed at his partner by the window. Ah God, the look of love on the man's face as he looked across to the woman with the bright red lips, sitting in her wheelchair. Amanda wanted someone to look at her that way. She had to call him twice, to break his reverie, and there was something spell-binding about the woman that Amanda wanted to get closer to.

Amanda drifted. Antony never looks at me like that. Adam called me honey, I touched his arm. He smiles at me.

Like a hand-maiden she had served the couple their drinks on a tray, and Adam was at the table beside them so that was nice, seeing him there as well. And when the woman spoke to her, with words she could no longer remember but just her beautiful voice, Amanda had felt a deep run of something flow through her like a thread of hot silver, coiling from deep inside her; some elemental thing like a curl of flame in a fire.

When she walked away from them, Amanda knew they were all watching her, Adam too, and she held her head high. She felt proud to be watched by them, even if she was their prey; and felt some visceral prickle on her skin at the back of her neck, three sets of eyes watching her, undressing her as she walked. She liked the pull of their eyes dragging cloth from her flesh as she walked. Amanda wanted to stand naked before them, her slim waist tapering to her taut ass and firm thighs. She was younger than they were, and would entice them. Their fingers would play with her breasts.

The train lurched and Amanda jerked awake, startled. She quickly looked around the carriage but nobody had noticed anything. The other passengers were heads down in their phones or trance like, gazing out the windows or seeing mirrors. Amanda's nipples were full and tight, and when the train rocked, the graze of her bra against her breasts was an exquisite rub. The tips of her nipples felt like ice, hot and cold at the same time, piercing her breasts. God, she thought, what's going on with me?

Amanda took another quick look around the carriage (good, nobody watching), then tightened her stomach muscles, pulling her belly flat. She quickly dipped a finger down inside her panties, her bag hiding the movement. Jesus, I am so wet, she thought. How long before the train gets in? Fuck, I hope no-one's in when I get home, I need to lock my door and make myself come. Why am I so horny? He calls me honey and looks at me with his deep blue eyes, and I touched his shoulder. What, Adam? No, I'm young enough to be your daughter.

And the woman with the luscious red lips, with her full pregnant belly, she talked to me and the beautiful man loves her. Why won't someone look at me like he looks at her? But Adam, he looks at me. He's old enough to be my father. Oh, but he looks at me, with a soft gentle look. He indulges me.

The train lurched across the crossing, the bells clanging, and shuddered and juddered to a stop. Amanda, her senses all jangled and an ache deep in her belly, stood and gripped the back of the seat. She shook her head and her pony tail flicked. Quick, she thought, get to my car, get home. Nobody be home, please, nobody be home.

As Amanda walked quickly across the car park, a last practical thought crossed her mind. God, my feet are sore. But it didn't matter because her nipples were tight and her pussy was wet, and she'd feel wonderful soon. She was so aroused from her dreams, faces blurring through the visions of her mind, that she stumbled.

Amanda drove home, her mind still fuzzy from day-dreaming in the train. It was most unusual for her to get so aroused on her own. Most nights it took a little persuasion from Ant for her passion to rise, she was so tired. Weekends were sweet though, sleepy mornings and slow waking, her long hair splayed wide on her pillow as he entered her. She would lift her legs and wrap them around his torso, she loved to be spread wide under him, her arms wrapped tight around his back, pulling him in.

But now, she just wanted her own fingers, fast and efficient, slow and meandering. When Amanda masturbated alone, she was fascinated by the way her mind wandered, shifting fantasies and images of strangers and lovers. And her own pace and flow. Sex with Ant was good, he was a sweet boy, but he often left her behind. When he came, he was gone too soon, leaving her alone in her bed. By herself, she always came.

I'm still warm in my bed. Goodness, Adam's words sounded in her head, and Amanda saw his wide shoulders, his creased blue eyes gazing fondly down at her. She liked his lop sided smile and a picture of him formed in her mind. No, she thought, that's too strange, he's too old for me. The memory of the younger man with his beloved woman flickered through her mind's eye, and the woman's red lips were so full and enticing. Amanda's nipples ached, there was too much going on in her head.

Pulling up in the drive of her house, she was pleased to find she was the first home. Good, the other girls were still at work, and Antony was at his place tonight. My time, thought Amanda, as she unlocked the front door. Going to her room, she kicked off her practical flat work shoes and collapsed on her back on the bed. My feet are so sore from standing all day, she thought. She lay there for a few minutes, just stopping from her long day. It was warm, the late afternoon sun warming her body as she dozed.

A flash of colour flickered in the tree branches just outside the window. A pair of rosellas landed on a branch, then flew off. Amanda went to the window to watch them go, bending down to massage her feet. Oh, that felt so good. She wiggled her toes in pleasure, then reached under her skirt to pull her hose and panties down. She smiled as she untangled her plain cotton-tails from the black nylon. Wow, the glamorous underwear of a working girl! She wondered what the women ordering coffee wore under their crisp, executive blouses. Crisp executive lingerie, she thought, whatever that looked like. Or felt like, on their skin.

Amanda flopped back into her bed, sliding up the length of it until her back lay against piled pillows. She reached behind her head and coiled her long hair high, but was too lazy to pull the band from her hair. She smiled at her own laziness, and the idea that her hair looked the same as her customers saw it popped into her head. Her customers didn't see her slowly closing eyes though, nor the red tip of her tongue licking her lips. They might have seen a faint flush of red at the base of her throat, sometimes, if they caught her distracted.

She stretched her limbs like a cat does, pointing her toes down the bed, her ankles touching; her arms outstretched and her fingers laced together. Her legs fell slightly apart, and her nipples tightened. Amanda pulled a long breath deep into her lungs, rising her belly high with the depth of it, then let it go with a sigh. Slowly the tension of the day left her, and her limbs warmed and relaxed even more. She opened her eyes, and the colours in her room seemed brighter, more alive. Ah yes, this little time to herself felt good.

Amanda's fingers wandered to the waistband of her skirt, and she pulled down the zip at the side. She shimmied the tight cloth down her thighs, lifting her legs from the covers then tugged the skirt away, dropping it to the floor.

The bed cover was soft and warm on the backs of her thighs and the cheeks of her ass. She wriggled, spreading her thighs wider. A coolness flowed between her legs as her pussy opened to the air. Amanda's eyes closed, and her fingers wandered to the base of her belly, her hand curving over the little delta of soft, dark hair. She loved the soft tickle against her palm, and pressed on herself.

Her skin was soft, and she shivered as her fingers wandered, finding that special place just inside her hip. Oh yes, the shiver rippled through her, and her nipples grew harder. She loved their tightness, and ached for her own touch on her breasts, but denied herself.

Oh my, she felt luxurious and spoiled, and didn't mind that it was her own touch on her flesh. Even though there was weightless air above her body, Amanda bent her legs up and pulled her thighs as high as she could. If it was Antony in the morning above her, she would open herself wide to him and taken his swift fuck into her. Ant was slight like her, slim and narrow hipped and she'd grip his body between her thighs wrapped tight.

But Ant wasn't there and she was heated still from her dreaming on the train. With her eyes closed she pictured first the beautiful man with the look of love in his eyes, but Amanda didn't know him. In his place she heard Adam's words and his voice; honey, he said, honey, and dipping between her legs there was honey, slick and warm between her lips and on her fingers.

Amanda's eyes were closed, but she saw his blue eyes smiling down at her. She knew his shoulders were broad in his suit, but she'd seen nothing else, so there in her head he was, leaning over her in a dark charcoal suit.

Her fingers dipped and slid, and Amanda swirled the nub of her clit in her own special way, gasping, oh fuck, fuck, moaning. She gripped the backs of her thighs with her hands and pulled them tight to her body, and her ass hole and sex were opening. Amanda gripped her firm ass cheeks and pressed a long middle finger to her hot, tight hole.

Her finger tip pressed, and she dipped it higher into the wet depth of her cunt until it was slick with her wetness. Pressing it back to her ass, the slickness was enough and her finger sunk to the second knuckle. Yes, yes, she wanted this, fuck me there, fuck me there. Ant, in my ass, fuck yes. But blue eyes gazed down on her and looked deep into her eyes. Oh fuck, Adam, she moaned, am I really your honey?

Now her fingers were sliding her lips wide, slicking moisture up over her clit. She rubbed her nub fast, faster, hitting perfectly the right places and pushing the heat in her belly till it throbbed. With little whimpers she stroked and pushed into herself, her sex wide and hot and wet, so wet. Ah yes, fuck fuck, she cried out, and she didn't know who was above her, whose face it was as she pushed herself up to a first, fast, climax.

Her nipples were tight ice, the friction of her twisting movement causing an exquisite pain, a wincing rub on the cloth of her bra. With a long moan followed by a low grunt, Amanda came again, her cunt throbbing. She clamped her thighs onto her hands, trapping her hands cupped between her legs. Her blouse twisted tight around her middle, bunched up exposing the base of her belly to the air. Her body shivered and jerked and Amanda shuddered with little aftershocks.

Ohh fuuuck that was good. She sighed, and pressed her hand hard between her legs. Her palm was hot slick with her wetness, and she cupped her sex like a little fallen bird, holding its fluttering heat in the cradle of her fingers. Oh fuck, his voice was soft, he called me honey and I touched his arm. Ant, where were you, why don't you look at me like that? Her dreaming men blurred and merged and mingled and her boyfriend wasn't amongst them. They looked at her with gentle, lovely faces, fondness in their eyes.

For several minutes Amanda lay there, her body hot in the early evening air. She grew cooler, and rolled herself into her bed under her covers and was warm, her hand still cupping her sex. I'm still warm in my bed, there was his voice. Amanda smiled, and two minutes later, she was asleep. Amanda dreamed, but when she awoke, she didn't know who had been in her dreams.

The Art Gallery

"Hey, Amanda, how are you?"

"Adam, hello. I'm well, thanks. Finished work for the day, thank goodness. You're off early too?"

"Yes, I'm going to the Gallery, there's an exhibition I thought I'd go see."

Adam had left work half way through the afternoon, and as he passed the front door of the café, there was Amanda. They nearly collided as she came out the door, both smiling as they each did a little side step and pirouette on the pavement.

"Where are you off to?" Adam asked, as they both seemed to be going in the same direction.

"The station," Amanda replied, hitching her bag over her shoulder. "Then the train to the hills." She looked up at him, and her fingers twisted a flick of hair from her cheek.

"We could walk together, if you like. We both need to get to the Embankment."

"Why not," the girl replied, and they crossed the next street, side by side.

They made an easy conversation together, as they had each told the other little snippets of their lives over many mornings and the occasional lunch when Adam went to the café. Amanda had an open innocence that Adam liked, and to see a pretty girl smile, well, that made his day worthwhile.

After walking a block they came to another crossing. The lights were against them, and Adam jabbed the walk button. "I don't know why I do that," he said, "we're going to get the lights anyway, on the cycle."

"I know, it's funny how we do things to hurry ourselves up, when really we should be slowing ourselves down." She laughed. "Amanda the philosophical, that's me."

"Amanda the wise, more like. You balance Adam the cynic, that's me."

While there was an edge of banter to his words, Adam knew there was a truth to them. Maybe that was why he was fond of this girl, she was fresh and young and reminded him of promises. His own were long lost, hers were still to be made.

Amanda must have sensed the change in his mood, for she touched his arm. "No. I can't believe you're a cynic. You don't seem that kind of a man."

"So what kind of a man am I, do you think?"

"What kind of a man?"

"Yes, what kind of a man?" Adam was curious for her answer.

Amanda took two steps back, as if to look at him from a distance. She hung one hand on her hip, exaggerating her dancer's counterpoint stance, while her other hand supported her chin, the classic thinker's pose. She looked at Adam, as if scrutinising him for the first time. "What kind of a man? Hmmm, let me see."

Adam laughed at her playfulness. "Aren't the young meant to respect those older and therefore wiser? You're just taking the piss now."

"Who, me?" she replied, all innocence and wide eyed astonishment.

"Come on," he said, "there's the walk sign. Let's go."

This time on the crossing, Amanda came closer to him and looped her arm through his. Her gentle teasing had broken through Adam's seriousness, and it seemed a natural thing for her to do. He looked down at the vibrant girl beside him, so spontaneous, so fresh, and his heart opened to her.

"Are you in a hurry to get home?" He didn't want her to go.

"Not really, no," she replied. "Why?"

"Can I buy you a coffee, and we could go see the exhibition together? I'm sure you'd like it."

"That'd be lovely, yes, I'd like that. But what's the exhibition?"

"Hundred Years of Fashion. It's from the Tate."

"Really? That'd be cool, yes, I'd love to see it with you. Nobody's taken me to an exhibition before. Not since mum and dad used to take me to museums and stuff, anyway, when I was a kid." Her excitement bubbled.

In the end, they got to the gallery before they could find another coffee shop, so once Adam had bought the tickets, he took her to the gallery café.

"Somebody can serve you for a change," he said, as they found a table in the warm afternoon sun.

"That would be nice, yes." Amanda looked around, checking out the place with her critical waitress' eye. "It's got a much better view than our place, hasn't it."

"Yes, but the girl behind the counter isn't the prettiest in the room." Adam looked at Amanda, wanting her reaction, whatever it might be.

Amanda glanced over to the counter, and Adam watched her appraise the woman there the way women do, quickly and precisely, with a slight narrowing of the eyes. She then looked back at him, meeting his gaze with a directness of her own.

"Are you flirting with me, Adam?"

"I guess I am, yes. Do you mind?"

Amanda looked at him, her hands motionless on the table before her. She was silent for a moment, giving nothing away on her face, a stillness in her. Then, and Adam's pulse thumped as he saw it, she replied with just the slightest smile. "No. I don't mind at all. I like the way you pay me attention, actually. It's different. Ant doesn't do it."

Ant doesn't do it. With those words Amanda placed her relationship on the table, and with it a challenge. So, Adam thought, this girl wants to be the only girl in her man's world, but she doesn't always get what she wants. Intriguing.

Now it was his turn to look at her silently, his hands motionless on the table before him. Adam didn't use words to reply, he didn't always need words. He lifted his hand from the table and with one finger pushed a tiny coil of hair away from her cheek, for surely it was tickling her skin and annoying her, just a little bit, and needed to be moved. I have to be so, so careful with this girl, he thought, she's like a wild thing, she can't be tamed. But she can be seduced, slowly, with great care and attention. If she'll let me.

Across the room, the woman behind the counter looked up. Something was crackling through the room, some elemental force. She saw them by the window, and smiled. The moment was intense, a slow conflagration, she could almost see the smoke rise. Surely the eyes of everyone in the room were drawn by this tiny fragment of time upon which anything and everything might turn, spiralling inwards and outwards at the same moment, demons dancing on a pin, angels falling.

Lucky girl, the older woman thought, she's found a man who has learned over time to wait, to pause. I'll give them a moment, then I'll take their coffee. I wonder what kind of a man he is. If the girl is very lucky, he's a slow, patient man who takes his time. She's still young, she's got plenty to learn.

Amanda shivered. Even though the table was warm in the sun, when Adam touched her cheek, so gently, so very gently, goose bumps ran up her arms. The deliberate act of possession in his touch astonished her. Amanda's men, until now, were all young and none had the confidence, nor the audacity, to claim ownership of her the way Adam had in that simple touch. Amanda felt she had been claimed by him, and she should have been offended. But he had been so gentle, so very gentle, and she craved the attention he gave her.

Antony never looked at her the way Adam did. Antony's look was distracted, fleeting, always somewhere else. He would get up and leave her longing, go gaming with his mates, reach for his phone. Sometimes she felt that Ant would do anything rather than talk to her; and emotion? None, really, that she could see. Not what she wanted, anyway.

But Adam. His gaze when he looked at her was so serious, so unyielding, yet so full of fondness and affection for her, she ached for it. When he spoke to her, it was as if nobody else was there, she was the only person in the room for him. For those moments, she felt as if she was the only woman in his world, that he needed her, wanted her. In those moments Adam adored only her, and oh goodness, she loved that. To be the centre of attention for five minutes, ten, Amanda wanted it.

But no, Adam is old enough to be my father, she dwelled on that. But is that it, to be loved like a daughter, unconditionally, is that it? But she wasn't his daughter, she knew that, there would be conditions. Then Amanda realised she too could have her own conditions. She might want to be seduced - she was coming to realise that's what was starting here, a seduction - but she could name her own conditions, couldn't she? But who was seducing whom?

She pondered her flirting with him. Was she leading him on, teasing him with her youth, her innocence, her freshness? She knew she was a girl with all of those delights. If he was too old, was she too young? Amanda didn't know what to think. She remembered an earlier afternoon, after she got home from dreaming on the train. Oh my, she thought, he calls me honey, and I tasted myself, and I was sweet as honey. A deep heat flooded into the base of her belly and oh sweet Jesus, the tips of her breasts ached and tightened. Oh fuck, the ache of that memory, that sweet coming, flooded into her cunt and she opened there.

She was rescued from the intensity of her reaction by the woman serving their coffee. "Sir," she said, "your latte." Turning to Amanda she placed the cup precisely. "M'mselle, yours. Please enjoy. It is a day for it."

Amanda looked up. That was a curious comment, so precisely spoken. The woman looked down at her, gazing straight into her eyes, then looked down just a fraction. Amanda immediately realised the woman was looking at her mouth, at her slightly opened lips. The older woman smiled just a little, an unsaid message. Amanda felt like she was in some kind of a conspiracy, but she wasn't sure who was conspiring with who.

She glanced at Adam, knowing that he would have seen the exchange. He too was looking at her mouth. She clenched her thighs, keeping the heat there. Amanda wondered whether he would know the state of her. She wanted to be eaten, taken, possessed. Heat flowed through her veins. Damn him, she wasn't in control here. But Amanda, she thought, do you want to be in control?

Slowly, making sure she didn't show nerves, didn't seem rushed, Amanda lifted the coffee to her lips. It was a perfect temperature, and a perfect froth. Her lips were slightly parted and blooming redder with the heat. She knew too that she was opening between her legs, even if her knees were primly together under the table.

"So, Adam, does the coffee compare?"

Amanda knew Adam watched her walk from a table after serving, and expected him to do the same here, to follow this other woman with his eyes. But no, his gaze was on her, only her. Amanda saw a slow shift of his eyes from her mouth to her own eyes, and his eyes were the darkest blue she had ever seen them, almost steel grey.

"Ah, a comparison." He paused. "Yes, the coffee is good, well made." He looked over to the woman, and held his gaze on her for a long moment, before looking back to Amanda. "But no, there is no comparison. Everyone is different, everyone has some unique thing, some special thing."

He smiled at her, then, quite deliberately, his eyes never leaving hers, he dipped just the tip of his fore-finger to the froth on the side of her cup and lifted it to Amanda's lips, so close but not touching, poised there. Amanda had no choice - he was claiming her once again and she allowed herself to be claimed - she opened her mouth ever so slightly to allow the red tip of her tongue between her lips, and took the taste from his finger, her lips brushing his finger tip."Damn you, Adam," she whispered, "what gives you the right to do that?"

"You do honey, you give me the privilege of touching your, because you don't look away. Your pride is your magnificence, it's your best feature."

Sweet Christ, thought Amanda, he calls me honey and magnificent, and I've tasted my own honey thinking of him. The idea of her wet sex sent a jab of pain to her clitoris and her cunt felt wet and full. Her legs parted. How on earth was she going to walk through the exhibition beside him, with her hot sex and her clit tight? Every step would be sweet friction, sweet pleasure, sweet torment. Oh God...

"Come, let's get through the exhibition, while it's still light."

You bastard, she thought, you're reading my mind. I could come in a second, and you've only just touched my lips with your finger. Is this what you do, every time you buy a woman coffee? Your arrogance is astonishing. Fuck you, Adam, I won't be wrapped around your finger. Her eyes darkened, a black passionate fury narrowing her eyes.

Ah good, Adam thought, her passion is rising, she's going to fight me every step of the way. She doesn't know how beautiful she is when her heat rises, her wild beauty.

He looked at Amanda as she finished her coffee, and she was no longer the little coffee girl who took his money and smiled at him in the mornings. She didn't know it, not yet, but Adam would crawl on his hands and knees just to be near her. His old, jaded heart could beat again, if she would let him get near her. Her vitality flowed from her, and ripped through him. Adam imagined the tension that would be rippling through her slender body. He loved to see this slow awakening in a woman, as they came to him of their own will.

"Amanda..."

"Yes, I'm listening, Adam. Please, let me finish my coffee, and when I'm ready..."

Her words were fierce, but her body betrayed her. Adam could see the flush of her arousal at the base of her throat, and he'd seen her pupils dilate when he said the word 'come.'

His own nipples were hard with a tight, sharp pain behind his breast. He knew himself well enough to know that his arousal was heightened by her closeness and her subconscious reactions to his actions; so if his nipples were tight, hers too would be hard and pleasurable, aching for a touch. He quickly glanced down, but her coat was wrapped tight, hiding her breasts.

"OK. Now I'm ready, Mr Impatient." Amanda gathered up her bag from the floor. Before she could push her chair back, Adam stood and quickly moved behind her, so that he could give her the old-fashioned courtesy of easing her chair back. It disarmed her, as he knew it would. "Oh, no-one's done that for me before," she said, "I could get used to that."

"It's my pleasure," Adam replied, and they were friends again. Amanda looked up at him and lifted two fingers to his lips. He kissed them, and this time she claimed him, on her terms. They smiled at each other, each knowing what the other was doing. She had never been courted before, and Adam was a patient man. He loved being with her, she was so alive.

They made their way to the gallery, and, because it was a weekday and late afternoon, they had the exhibition mostly to themselves. Adam was content to place himself in front of each tableau and to soak in the luxury of it all, the flamboyance. He loved the genius of the couture, the brilliance of the colours and the superb embroidery.

In contrast to his stillness, Amanda circled the exhibits, seeing the clothing from all sides, even crouching down to see it from different angles.

"Adam, they're so beautiful." She'd return to his side with a breathless joy, as if to momentarily anchor herself, then dart off to another place, another time.

"Yes, they are beautiful clothes, aren't they. I can see why you like them." He looked down at the vivacious creature beside him, restless like a cat. "I've always thought that women dress to impress women..." He paused, "...and undress to impress men."

She looked up at him, taken by his comment. I wonder if I could impress him, she thought. She shook her head. No, don't be silly. He'd want someone older, surely.

"Oh look, I can imagine myself wearing that, dancing in some old smoky club!"

Adam sensed she was working off the nervous energy of her earlier arousal, and she would soon slow down and stop. Sure enough, after about twenty minutes, she found a bench and dropped herself onto it. "My poor feet, they're aching."

"Oh Amanda, I'm so sorry, I should have thought. You've been on your feet all day, and here I am, dragging you round an art gallery. You poor darling. Here, let me."

Adam sat a little distance from her, and tenderly lifted one of her feet to his lap, and took off the practical flat shoe. Amanda stretched out her toes in pleasure, leaning back at the same time to keep her balance, even before she realised what he was doing. He massaged her foot between his strong fingers, kneading the base of it.

"Oh God," she sighed, "that's wonderful. Please, don't stop."

Adam didn't stop, he kept massaging her foot, until suddenly she became self conscious. "Adam, no, stop. My foot, surely it's all hot and sweaty. You can't."

"Honey," and the endearment came so naturally to Adam, "if I didn't want to do this, I wouldn't. Surely you don't mind." It was a statement, not a question, and he didn't stop. "Your nylon stockings though..."

"They're not stockings, just plain, practical pantyhose. You don't like them, do you?"

"Well, they're not soft silk, and they're not warm skin, so I'll..."

"You'll do nothing. Stop, let go my foot." Amanda swivelled her feet to the floor and stood. She looked around, but they were alone in the gallery, and the bench was in a dark corner of the room. "Don't look."

Amanda quickly turned and raised up the hem of her plain black skirt, put both hands up to her waist, and peeled down the hose and her panties. Adam, not knowing what she was going to do, didn't look away, and was rewarded with a quick glimpse of a pale thigh. Turning back to him, she quickly rolled the flimsy garments into her hands, plunging them deep into her bag before he could really see. She primly smoothed down the fabric of her skirt, and was once more the neat, tidy, coffee girl in a simple black skirt. Slit cunt naked underneath, she was two girls in one; hot heat and slow arousal, pretty coffee girl and sensuous young woman, both.

Her eyes sparkled as she looked down at him. Adam was pleased, she's playing seriously now. She sat beside him on the bench, her back against the wall, and placed both feet in his lap. "Now, Adam, what were you saying about warm skin?"

Adam met her look. "My, you are a forward young miss, aren't you. What would your mother think?" His hands were warm and enclosed her foot like a cunt does a cock, gripping tight and not letting go.

"I'm not sure about my mother. But my old Gran always used to say, 'Amanda, always wear clean knickers. You never know when you might fall over in the street.' A wise old woman, my Gran." She grinned at Adam. "She'd always tell me, 'make sure you meet a nice young man, Amanda, but if his mother hasn't taught him manners, send him back home.'" She paused. "Did your mother teach you manners, Adam?"

"Hmmm, manners. I suspect not. Anyway, you're safe with me." He took her other foot into his hands. She didn't resist.

"Oh really, why is that?" She didn't want to resist.

"We're not in the street." Adam paused. "And I'm no longer young. I was a nice young man, once upon a time, or so I was told. But now, I'm just getting old."

Adam held her feet in his hands, and her skin was soft and warm. He caressed further up Amanda's calves, but even though he knew she was now bare under her black skirt, he wanted to wait, to draw out their teasing, to tantalise both himself and her. He was also intrigued to discover what Amanda might do, if left to her own devices. He was a patient man, and could wait to find out. He waited for the seduction, it would come, he was sure of that. He just wasn't sure who would seduce who. Amanda was learning fast, and had ideas of her own.

What in God's name am I doing, thought Amanda. I've taken my panties off in an art gallery, and a man who I sell coffee to is massaging my bare feet. That can't be right, but my feet feel sooo good, and Adam is so kind, buying me a ticket to the exhibition. And he's such good company. He pampers me. I love it, and he seems to enjoy it. But what am I doing?

Amanda laughed inside to herself, both at her conundrum and also in astonishment at herself for doing what she was doing. What would her old Gran think, indeed! She could imagine her shaky old voice: 'Amanda you really shouldn't take your knickers off in public. What would your mother think? Really, girl.' She giggled at her imaginary granny.

"Oh, I see," commented Adam, "there's something to laugh about now, is there?"

"God no, it's delicious, your hands on my poor tired feet. No, I was just imagining what my old Gran would be thinking, if she saw me now."

"You'd be surprised," Adam replied. "She'd probably say to you, 'if you're not in bed by eleven o'clock, go home.' That's what my old Nan said to me, when I was a teenager." He shuddered. "God, that's too long ago, to even think about."

She looked at him and wondered if he fully registered that he was talking about beds to a twenty-three year old. Surely he did? She'd tried to work out his age from things he had said, and from his appearance; and figured he must be somewhere in his fifties, with his silvery grey hair. She wondered at herself. An older man? His daughter could be my age.

Can it be right that I've taken off my panties and I've got my feet in his lap? I want him to touch my cheek again, and brush a tiny coil of my hair away. I want to touch his lips again with my fingers, I want to see his eyes narrow as they look me up and down, glancing at my breasts (does he like small breasts?). I want him to adore me.

Amanda looked at Adam, her eyes dark with passion, her mind slowly making itself up. She had her pantyhose and knickers in her bag, and was calculating how long at this rate it would be before all of her clothes were on the floor, in her bag, falling off her body. Shoes and underwear already; skirt, blouse, bra and coat still to go. Good God, she realised, that's four garments taken off already, four to go. Five, as she looked at her watch and included it in her calculation.

"Adam, how long have we been together this afternoon?"

He looked at his watch. That's curious, thought Amanda, he's right handed but he wears his watch on his right wrist. "Oh, I'd say an hour and a half, two hours. Why?"

"I'm just calculating how forward I am, given I've got my panties off and bare legs already, and it's still light outside."

"How forward you are?" Adam looked at her, and she melted. The smile in his eyes caught her heart and she adored him, then it tugged hot and cold behind her breasts and into her nipples and she craved for him; and his eyes narrowed and a silver thread wound around her clit and she lusted for him, her sex blooming open between her legs like a dark, fragrant flower. She couldn't do her maths fast enough.

"The question isn't how forward you are. The question is how forward I might be..."

Amanda tilted her head into the perfect angle for coy. "I hope..." and cleared her throat to make sure the words didn't falter, "I hope you listened to your Nan."

Under her feet she felt a slow shift as Adam's cock thickened. He looked at his watch again. "I did," he replied, "And I always paid attention to the time."

Adam kissed the tips of his fingers and put them to Amanda's lips, sealing a promise. "We've time for dinner, but not a movie." He said it as if it was a perfectly normal thing to do, to take in a movie with a friend after a long day at work.

"I don't want a movie," said Amanda, I want you. She left it unsaid, but hoped he heard her. She thought Adam was probably seducing her, but even so, she seemed to be making a lot of the moves. Is that the difference, she wondered, between someone who's probably done this a dozen times, and someone who's never done it even once? Finally, Amanda thought, I've found a man who knows what he's doing.

Poor Antony, he's not got a chance against Adam. The idea of her boyfriend, and what she was doing here, flickered across her mind but she thrust it away. Nothing's happened to feel guilty about, she thought, knowing full well it had. Like Scarlett, she could sort that out another day.

They got to their feet, Amanda reluctantly putting her shoes back on, and smoothing down her skirt. As she turned, Adam admired the way the cloth followed the tight contours of her bare ass. The crease between her cheeks and the long line of her thighs were unbroken by a panty line, and the skirt clung enticingly to her curves as she walked.

Amanda walked ahead of him, knowing he was watching the sway of her hips, her taut calves. She turned once to look over her shoulder, her long hair swirling, and beckoned him with her finger. "Come, Adam. Haven't you seen a girl's ass before?"

"Well yes, but can't I admire yours? It really is delectable."

"I know. Walking around all day really keeps me toned, don't you think?"

Amanda enjoyed their flirting back and forth, at the same time wondering what would happen when he got really serious. She imagined his intensity would overwhelm her, that she would be way out of her depth and swept away by him. Deep in her belly a pulse throbbed but she managed to keep her walk steady. Take a breath, Amanda, take a breath. How on earth am I going to last through dinner? she wondered.

As they walked out of the gallery, the woman in the café watched them go. She saw there was a perfect distance between them, not too close so that the girl was fawning on him or he was controlling her; and not too distant that they were remote and disconnected from each other. That's lovely, she thought, they are going into wherever they are going as equals. She had no doubt that the electricity between these two would surge like a storm before they were done with each other.

Amanda touched her hand to Adam's arm, wait. She turned and looked straight at the woman behind the counter, on the other side of the room, straight into her distant eyes. Some tiny bit of the witch in Amanda was drawn by the more practiced witch in the older woman, and across the ether there was a silent exchange between them both. Amanda now understood the strange comment the woman had made earlier. It was indeed a day for it.

The Hotel Room

Adam took her to a discreet low-key restaurant in the basement of a city hotel. At first, Amanda was self conscious about her simple attire, until Adam re-assured her.

"You're fine. When you're sitting, anyone else will see just a young woman in a white blouse, the rest of you is hidden under the table. It's early evening, so you could easily pass for a young staff officer on an interstate visit, being taken out by a manager from another company."

Adam sat across from her, so they were formal, close but not intimate. Discretion was a simple thing to arrange.

"Besides," Adam went on, "I've only ever seen you in your work clothes, so if I'm to undress you later I'll find out whether you are as lovely as my imagination says you will be. Tonight, I can't imagine you in anything else."

He said it as if it was the most straightforward thing in the world, that she would be undressed later. Amanda had gone well beyond her original reaction to his confidence, which she had thought was arrogance, and now she just wanted to be the centre of his slow, steady seduction as he teased it out.

She replayed his words in her mind. 'If I'm to undress you later.' She loved the idea of Adam slowly, carefully removing her clothing, one item at a time, revealing her young body as a prize. She could imagine the look on his face as she was exposed in her lovely, naked glory. She would turn around slowly in front of him so he could see her from every angle. She would pull the band from her high ponytail and let her hair fall. He would touch her bare skin with his lips and worship her.

The meal was wonderfully prepared, perfect sized portions leaving her comfortably full. They shared a single bottle of wine, which meant Amanda was warm and relaxed, but not at all drunk. Good, she thought, I won't do anything embarrassing. She was nervous though. What if he thought she was too young, too inexperienced? Even if she was young and fresh, might he want someone older, more knowing? Sometimes she felt like a silly school girl, terrified that she would say something so stupid, so naive, that he would just walk away.

"Adam, I just wanted to say..."

"Sshh, Amanda, no need to say anything. Everything's fine. More than fine, it's perfect. You're a beautiful young woman, it's my privilege to be seen with you. Now, may I get you desert?"

"No, thank you. I've had the perfect amount to eat. Thank you so much for dinner, it was wonderful." You're wonderful, she thought, but can I say that to you? Instead, she reached out and touched two fingers to Adam's cheek, so lightly it was almost as if she was afraid to touch him, for fear he would vanish perhaps, just a dream.

Adam leaned ever so slightly into her touch, and her palm held the side of his face in a gentle caress. He might undress her later, but she could care for him too.

"Adam, take me upstairs, please. I don't want to wait any longer. Can I be your woman, now?"

He smiled at her; and between her legs her bare sex bloomed, and under her plain white blouse, cupped inside her practical white bra, her nipples throbbed and tightened. Feeling the pressure on her breast, she reached inside the neck of her blouse and adjusted the thin strap of the bra, pulling up the weight of her hot flesh. She wanted to press her hand against her breast and feel the hard heat of her thick bud against her palm, but she was in a public place, and couldn't do that.

She shook a little as she stood, and leaned her hand on the table.

"Are you OK, my love?" asked Adam, and gave her a new title. It was such a precious thing, his anointment of her.

My love. Ohhh, thought Amanda, I've never been anybody's love before. Does he know what his words do to me? "Yes, I'm OK, I just stood too quickly, I'm fine, really."

"Walk with me, Amanda, walk beside me."

In the lift, they stood side by side, not touching. Adam's cock was thickening and he was pleasantly aware of himself as he looked down at the young woman beside him. Amanda focused on the heat in the depth

42

of her belly, and she was wet. She looked up at his silvering hair and wondered if it was the same colour on his chest. He's old enough to be my father. The thought flashed through her mind. But he's not my father, and the thought was gone.

The lift opened, and they were alone in the corridor. Amanda reached for his hand, and Adam's strong, warm fingers wrapped around hers. Or Adam reached for her hand, and she slipped her slim fingers into his. Was he leading her, or was she leading him? No matter, hands were held and those little movements between them were all that mattered.

At the door of their suite Amanda stood back as he placed the card into the slot, and with a solid click, the door opened. Inside, a single lamp beside the bed illuminated the room. At the window, the curtains were open, and they looked down over the sparkling lights of the city. A tram slid past, blue flashes arcing from its wire.

Amanda placed her coat on a chair and turned to him, wanting to be directed now, taken, led by the hand. She knew that she was the innocent one, now that the seduction had moved past flirting (she could do that); moved past small talk in a café (she managed that nicely); and had progressed past the wine and the meal. Amanda placed herself in his hands. I'm safe there, she thought.

Adam took her by the hand once more and lead her to the window. He knelt beside her and removed first one shoe then the other. "Your poor feet, they must be aching, it's been a long day for you."

He stood up behind her. She was small and slight before him, and she rested her head on his shoulder, leaning back slightly. Adam kissed her hair, and reached for the band that held her high ponytail in place, and carefully pulled it up and away from her head. Her long hair fell, and he arranged it so it fell down one side of her body, its length twisting through a long spiral. He placed one hand on her belly and held her in front of him, his other hand holding hers.

Amanda knew that he was in no hurry, and began to luxuriate in his every slow movement. God on earth, where had he learned such patience? Between her legs she was wet, so very wet. Yet he just held her belly, and it was her sexiest place. Against her hip, Amanda felt a shift of flesh, and she pushed back gently against a thickening heat. Her mind raced, trying to imagine his cock, what it would look like, what it would feel like in her hand, what it would taste like in her mouth.

She licked her lips, and her cunt throbbed. His slow, silent cupping of her belly was so intimate, so personal, and her senses heightened. The lights outside seemed sharper, brighter, and she heard distant sounds from the street below. She felt a pulse in her throat. She felt his thickening behind her.

Adam left one hand gently cupping Amanda's belly, which had a lovely curve to it, a little roundness. He moved his other hand up to her throat and undid the buttons of her blouse, one by one, moving slowly down the centre of her. Amanda wondered how his fingers could be so dexterous, until she looked at the window. Her focus shifted, and she saw that the light in the room came from such an angle that the window was like a mirror. She could see them both clearly, reflected there, and saw that Adam was watching his own fingers.

Adam undid every button on the blouse, and placed his warm hands directly on her skin. He reached inside the opened side of her blouse, and cupped a breast, the soft cloth of the bra under his palm. God, he's so gentle with me, Amanda thought. Every touch of me is the most caring, most precious thing in the world, it's like everything about me is worshipped and sacred.

She wanted to be naked in front of him, exposed in her young beauty. She moved away a little, and quickly dropped the blouse from her arms, letting it drop to the floor. While she was in motion, and momentarily out of Adam's arms, she slipped the thin straps of the bra from her shoulders, turned the garment around her torso and unclipped the clip. It too fell to the floor, and she stood there, half turned towards Adam, dressed only in her black skirt.

Adam gazed at her naked breasts, unashamedly looking at her, absorbing her dark areola and her long, thick nipples. Amanda wanted the heat of his mouth to suck her nipples harder, but not yet. She smiled up at him, as if to say, you like? She knew damn well that he did, that her body was lithe and slender before his eyes, and her back was slim. She saw his eyes narrow with lust and desire. She took her long hair in a twist, and it fell and covered one breast. She could be artful too, arranging herself as a vision before his eyes.

She slid down the zip of her skirt, and it too fell in a coil around her ankles. Amanda was completely nude before him, but wasn't at all self conscious. She bent down to pick up all of the clothes she had dropped, and the firm flesh of her ass was displayed for his delight. Her small breasts dropped to long points as she bent over. Adam watched as she unabashedly picked up her clothes, turned to a chair, neatly folded the garments and placed them on it.

She looked at him again, and her eyes were black and wide, her smile confident, her lips full. Amanda loved being naked, nude, in front of this man, and he drank her in. She reached her arms up and wide to grip the curtains. As she pulled them together, she turned and wrapped them around her, so only her face showed.

"Adam, can you run me a shower, please. I'd love a shower before I go to bed." It was her turn to talk about bed now, as she teased him with the sight of her delicious body, before hiding it away, fleeting glimpses. His slow seduction gave her a new confidence, and she loved revealing herself and hiding herself.

"Of course, my love. And I'll dry you with a big towel when you're done." He turned towards the bathroom, shedding his jacket and placing it on the bed as he went past. Her naked beauty enticed him, excited him, but he could wait. Amanda would be a great delight, not to be rushed. With women, Adam had learned to be slow and careful. Hard and fast when the time was right for it, but not yet for this girl. Softness first, with this girl.

He ran the shower, and as Amanda walked past him into the bathroom, beautifully nude, she reached up to his face and kissed him once on the lips. She couldn't stop smiling. She wanted this man so much, but she too could wait. She wanted to imagine him, as he had imagined her, then watch him undress. When she was ready.

She wrapped her hair up into a plastic cap, then stepped into the shower, knowing he was watching her every move. She deliberately ignored him, paying attention only to herself, lathering her body with the lightly scented soap. The water ran. He went back to the bedroom, wanting her so much.

She called him. "Adam, come dry me, I'm done." She stood on the floor towel, waiting for him, water beading down her skin. He wrapped her close in a big towel, and dried every limb, her front and back, between her legs.

"How can you be so gentle?" she asked, loved and caressed by his strong hands. Sex itself was a distant promise right at that moment, but Adam drying her was so erotic, so tender, so full of affection.

"I've had small children," he replied, "you learn to care utterly for a small child." He patted her back dry with the towel, wrapping it around her. "When you've cared for a child, it's just... well, you never forget how to do it. You make me remember that caring."

Adam looked at her with a flicker of emotion crossing his face. His eyes were bright. "Amanda, you've brought something out in me that I've not felt for a long time."

He was kneeling beside her, and she looked down at his upturned face. "Oh, Adam, what should I do?"

He smiled up at her, and looked a little lost. "You'll know. When it's time, you'll know. Women always know." He stood. "But now, miss, make yourself comfortable on the bed, in the bed. It's my turn for a shower." He reached behind the door. "Here, put this dressing gown on." He laughed, "God, you're adorable. It's so big on you, where have you gone?" Her lovely face was all he could see of her, the gown so long and luxurious, nearly wrapped around her twice.

Amanda wanted to watch him strip, to see his tall frame in the shower, but she had been directed to bed, in the bed, on the bed. Adam was making it her choice about the next moment, the next five minutes, the next hour. She had to decide so many things for him, for them. On the bed or in the bed?

She thought of the curators at the gallery and their artistry - how best to array the clothing, how to show it in its glory. She too must treat herself like a work of art, and make their first moment together timeless.

She smiled to herself as she made her way to the bed, pondering her best angles, wondering what his favourite curves might be. How could she surprise Adam and delight him. On the bed or in the bed?

In the shower, Adam soaped his body all over. The nice thing about us both having a shower, he thought, is that we've both used the same soap. This means we'll easily be able to distinguish each other's scents and tastes, untainted by any other perfumes or powders. His cock began to thicken as he remembered the smell of an aroused woman, that slightly metallic taste of her cunt when she came. He knew the taste of his semen had a little sweetness to it, and hoped Amanda would like it.

He wondered where Amanda might take him. He knew at some time he would come inside her; but whether he would come in her mouth or somewhere on her skin, well, that would depend on the course of events, what she liked.

Adam pondered the girl, the young woman in the room beyond. He loved her spirit and her bright intelligence. Finding someone his intellectual match was always a pleasure. Her independence too, he admired that. Over the course of the afternoon and evening her moods had shifted and ebbed, and he supposed his had too. Amanda understood stillness and silence, which suited him. Words weren't always needed.

He stepped out of the shower and dried himself. He looked down at his body. Not too bad, for a man in his fifties. Not as taut as when he was a young man, true, but he swam several kilometres a week and was in reasonable shape. His cock was thick but not hard, and swung pleasingly against his left thigh. His balls were loose from the heat of the shower, but never hung low. Adam cupped them in his hand, and they were cool in his palm. Ah yes, he thought, the hot and cold of a man.

He reached for another robe from the back of the door, and wrapped it around himself. He could take it off later, when she wanted to see all of him.

Adam opened the door of the bathroom, and saw that Amanda had pulled back the curtains a couple of feet. A full moon cast a pale light through the room. The bedside lamp was lit, spreading a warmer glow. Amanda lay on the bed, still in her robe. She had arranged the pillows behind her back and was half sitting, half lying on the bed, with the covers pulled back. She was like an odalisque in a classical painting.

But both feet were together and pointing towards Adam, her toes straight up. She wriggled them in a hello, and it was such a silly, delightful gesture that Adman had to laugh. Amanda wasn't treating this seduction with the gravitas it never deserved, she was playful and making it fun. Somewhere she had learned that sex with joy is best.

"Adam, my feet are saying hello, because you paid them so much attention, earlier on." Amanda's voice was light, her eyes bright and smiling. Then her voice lowered, and the exquisite sexiness that he sometimes heard at the coffee counter was there.

"But stop right there. Your gown, take it off. I want to look at you. I've only ever seen you in a suit."

Beneath his gown, Adam's cock throbbed. He had no problems, none whatsoever, with Amanda telling him what to do. He could see from her intense gaze that he was going to be scrutinised, held naked in front of her. He undid the robe and let it fall to his feet, but didn't move. He held his hands loosely by his sides, and stood, letting her study him.

Amanda looked at his face, those familiar eyes and the slight crooked smile. Adam's hair was slicked back, still wet from the shower, and silver in the moonlight. The hair on the top half of his chest was silvered too, darkening into blackness on his belly. Amanda took a quick intake of breath when her gaze travelled over his hanging thickness, and she saw even when soft his cock was long. It was beautifully proportioned, not too thick and not too thin, its head still mostly covered by its foreskin.

Her mind went to the only other cock she knew really well, and she knew immediately that Antony's shaft, even when hard, was shorter than the one before her now. She'd never much thought of different sized cocks before, but Adam...

"Closer, step closer. I want to see you closer."

Adam took two steps towards the bed, and was rewarded by Amanda pulling back the sides of her bath robe, revealing her nude body, legs slightly parted now. She rested one hand along the top of her hip, her fingers pointing straight at the dark cleft between her thighs. Her neat triangle of hair was like a shadow on the base of her belly. Amanda's nipples were tight, her slight breasts high on her chest.

Adam looked upon her, and his cock stirred and thickened at the sight of her.

"Oh, so you like what you see, then." Amanda had seen his silent response, and was delighted that her young body could instantly provoke a thickening.

"Oh yes, I like what I see very much. Very much indeed."

"Well, don't just stand there. Come to the bed, come to me." There, Amanda had said it, she'd invited him to her bed. Their bed, in their room, in their small city. I wonder how many other couples are going to their beds right now, Amanda thought. How many are like me, doing this for the first time?

Adam went to the side of the bed, leaned over and kissed her. For the first time, he kissed Amanda fully and deeply on the lips, tasting her sweet skin and teasing her tongue with his. She kissed him back, and both her hands went to the back of his head. "Ohhh, Adam, quick, lie down here, hold me."

She couldn't help her eagerness, turning on her side to hold him close. She ran her hands through the hair on his chest, and rested one palm over his heart. She dragged her fingers over his nipple, and it was tight and pointed. She pressed her hand against it, and felt a hot movement against her thigh. "Adam, fuck, your cock. I love your cock, show me your cock." She pushed him onto his back.

"Whoa girl, slow down," Adam reached for her, cradling her cheek in the palm of his hand. "There's plenty of time to meet my cock, there's no hurry." But he loved it that she wanted his hard cock, and her voice when she said it: cock, cock, fuck that was sexy. He pushed back on a button, testing for a reaction. "Show me your tits and cunt, and you can touch my cock. How's that for fair."

Amanda pulled herself up the bed until one pert tit was near his mouth. "That's fair, here, suck on this," she said, as she dropped her breast to his mouth. At the same time, she swung a leg over Adam's torso and ground her wet cunt against his side. Her grip was tight, her lithe legs wrapping around his. "I'm so fucking horny." She sounded a little surprised at herself.

Adam was fully erect now, the unexpected words coming from her mouth causing his prick to bounce and tighten. Wow, I didn't expect that, he thought, I figured she might be more reserved. She's a changeling. "Suck me, Amanda, take my cock into your mouth."

"Wait, Adam. When I'm ready, I'll suck you. You have to pamper my nipples first. My breasts and nipples are so sensitive. I think it's coz my tits are small."

"Amanda, your breasts are perfect. You're going to love your small breasts when you're forty, that's for sure."

Does he mention the age thing deliberately, Amanda wondered, because of the difference in our ages, or because he's older and can think of women at different ages, because they're all around him, they're who he sees? She couldn't imagine being forty, it was just too far away. She started to picture the different women who came into the café, how they dressed, how they carried themselves, how they looked. She realised her youth was a fleeting thing.

"Amanda, honey, where have you gone? You're not here." Adam instinctively circled his arm around her back, pulling her head back down to his shoulder and cradling her delicate body against his. Her mood had suddenly shifted, and he sensed that his silence was the best thing. She probably couldn't say what it was, if he asked her.

He cradled her head against his chest, stroking her hair, calming her. She was like a cat, letting herself be calmed. He smiled. She's been aroused for hours, he thought, remembering that lovely, quick flash of her thigh as she pulled her panties down her legs. Was that today? It seemed like ages ago.

He was big in the bed, and warm. With her cheek against his chest, a hair tickled Amanda's nose, and she brushed it away. Adam's heart beat was slow and steady. As she lay there, she heard, every ten beats or so, a slight pause and a quick catch up. It was as if his heart was almost missing a beat, then deciding, yes, that's the right time, that's the beat, keep going.

His hand through her hair was soothing, and she was conscious of his other hand just resting on her hip, not moving. She threaded her fingers through the hair on his chest and was content, pressing rhythmically with her finger tips against his skin. Her eyelashes flickered, tension fell away and she softened onto his body. He's so comforting, she thought, as she drifted into the sensation of his hand stroking her hair.

Amanda's body jerked, and a little sigh came from her lips. Adam stopped stroking her hair for a moment, listening for her movement, her breath. Gently, he pulled one of the bed covers over them, to keep her warm. As he lay there, he listened to the low hum of the air conditioner and the distant noises from the street below, and the soft sound of Amanda's breathing. His heart melted, and he held her safe.

Amanda shifted a little, moving herself up a few inches. Reaching up to his face, she slowly ran her fingers around his cheek, then traced the curve of his lips. He's got luscious, full lips, I want to bite them like a strawberry. Her other hand slowly moved down over his belly to touch the heat of his cock, god it's so hot, she thought, his flesh is so hot. She measured the length of him with her out-stretched hand, from the tip of her thumb to the end of her little finger. She checked the same length on his belly, and the tip of his cock nearly touched his navel. "So long," she whispered, "how will it fit?"

Adam smiled at her movements and her measurement of him. His cock bounced against her hand and she gripped him. One hand gripped him and the other touched his cheek, and their energy started to circulate with a tantric intensity. Adam knew the subtle power of breath, and let flow a low moan from deep in his throat.

Her body shivered at the sound, and her fingers tingled. With one hand at the back of Amanda's head, he pulled her lips to his; and his other hand drifted to the base of her spine and it was electric there.

Their kiss deepened, and with it their tongues touched and pushed. Her tongue became a tight, hard, insistent little fuck into his mouth and she took him. His hand on her spine pressed her body down on to his, and his fingers splayed over the cheeks of her ass, pressing, pressing her flesh. His hand covered one firm cheek and squeezed, and his other hand flowed down her body and he gripped both the firm moons of her ass.

Adam spread his hands, and the puckered bud of her asshole felt the cooler air, and the lips of her sex widened. Amanda moaned, and he swallowed her breath, her body twitched. Their breath grew rhythmic together, and their sexual energy intensified. Amanda didn't know this way of loving, but her body quickly tuned to his and her senses heightened. Ohhh, fuuuck, and her body jerked.

Her grip tightened on his shaft, ahhh, yes, his cock. Her cunt bloomed, and she pressed her wet lips against his hip. Her body twitched and her mouth went dry, and she gasped her throat open for breath. His breath took hers and gave it back, and he pulled her small frame tight against his. Her sex pressed to his hip. Her hand tried to stroke his shaft, but she couldn't concentrate. Adam's mouth took her breath and gave it back.

Her other hand gripped the sheets, she couldn't breathe, he breathed into her and their energy spiralled. Amanda's eyelids fluttered, she'd never had sex like this before and they were only breathing. Sweet Jesus, her cunt opened and she was so wet, she'd never been this wet before, and suddenly she was crying.

Amanda pushed herself up, her arms outstretched so she could gaze down on Adam's face below her. Her eyes were wide open, big black pupils pulling the light of his face into her mind. Tears streamed down her cheeks as emotions thrilled through her. Her lips were full, red, hot with blood and passion, and her mouth was beautiful for Adam to see.

"How... how... how is it you can do this to me? I'm bliss... God, I've never felt this before. Fuck, look, my whole breast feels like the tightest, hottest nipple I've ever felt." Amanda looked down at her breast, and her nipple was hard and thick, pulling out the flesh of her breast to a tight point. "It doesn't look bigger, but it's all I can feel."

Adam reached his open hand up to her breast, cupping it, pushing it, feeling her heat. She shuddered, a ripple of ecstasy surging through her. She pressed her own hand against his on her breast, and their rising sexual energy coursed between them.

Adam's eyes too were deep and black, his pupils streaming in, pulling in the light of her, her beauty. He adored her as she graced him with her loveliness, her joy, her innocence. And he wasn't even inside her yet. They gazed deep into each other's eyes, connecting, connecting, joining together, and their hearts rushed.

"Every woman, Amanda, every woman who ever taught me, it's in my hands, what I learned." He reached for her cheek, touching the track of her tears with the tip of his finger and claiming the salt for himself. "Everything I've learned from women, it's in my hands."

She smiled down at him, and touched his lips with a finger. "So you think you know something about women, then?"

"No, nothing at all. I still need to be taught."

There was a silence in the room as Amanda took in what he was saying. She shifted her body on his, wriggling down an inch or two. "Teach me what you know, then, from these women." She kissed him, hard. "Teach me what you know."

On a bed in a room in a small southern city, Adam remembered; and the memory was in his fingertips and his breath and his long, hot heat. Amanda sighed with the pleasure of them, oh my sisters, you taught him well. And she hadn't taken him inside herself yet.

"Did they teach you this?" she whispered, aligning her body with his, lying on top of him, feeling the long hot heat of him against her belly. "Don't move. Don't you dare move." Her eyes were black and her lips were red and her cunt was so, so wet.

Amanda shifted her weight upon him, and deliberately moved one thigh then the other so she could hold him still. She reached down between their bodies to perfectly align the tip of him with the petals of her, and circled a wetness around them both. While her hand was there, she pressed her favourite fingers to her clit, and circled there. She shuddered, and the arousal that had been building all afternoon climbed higher. She followed it.

Slowly, oh so fucking slowly, Amanda lowered herself onto his shaft, inch, fuck, yes, inch by slow hot thick inch. She bit her lip with a fierce concentration, and Adam held the back of her head in both his hands, pulling her long hair to one side. With each slow inching slide her wetness slicked and slipped, and her cunt gripped him.

"Don't move," Amanda whispered, "just me, just me. Oh fuck, slide into me." She shivered. "Oh sweet goodness."

Adam's body quivered, and she gripped him and stopped her slow fuck onto him. With her finger on his lips, shhh, stop, don't come, she slowed him. Beautiful man, not yet. Me first, just me. After some seconds, certain of him and so very sure of herself, Amanda opened and opened and opened above him and took him in and his cock was deep inside her and she slid down around him, every long, slow inch taken, taken, taken inside her. Amanda stopped, and was silent and still, her body all a long cunt all around him and he was inside her, his heat in her, and she gripped him.

Ah, sweet fuck, she took his face in both her hands like her gospel. Seeing nothing else but his dark eyes, no blue but blackness in the cool moon light, Amanda held his face, and with one last grip to slow him, the lips of her sex were hot against the risen coolness of his full balls and his shaft was deep and thick inside her. She stilled herself, and felt a pulse within her that was not hers.

"Adam," she whispered, "it's time. Can I be your girl?"

Adam could feel her quivering around him, her body edged to the height of the tallest cliff, ready to fly and fall, peaking and peaking and wanting him.

"Ah, honey, be my woman," Adam answered, and the words were enough.

Amanda's eyes widened in surprise and her mouth opened in silence as her orgasm ripped through her, her arousal since her fury at him in the café finally releasing after the long hours of tension. She shuddered and came, waves of pleasure surging up and down her spine, her cunt pulsing around his heated shaft.

Adam fucked up into her, pushing his long cock deep and she took him, her throbbing orgasm clenching him long and hot into her. He held himself back from coming, so he could savour her sweet release. Amanda lay on him, straightening her legs and tightening her grip on his heat, and she was lovely, slender and slight. He held her close in his arms, loving the lightness of her body. Aftershocks rippled through her, and he held her. Adam wrapped his arms around her and held her back, feeling her muscles flutter.

Amanda buried her lips against Adam's throat, kissing him there and cradling his head in her hands. She lifted her head up a little, and kissed his lips, his cheek, his eyelids. She propped herself up on one arm and gazed down at him, and was lost in his eyes. I'm his honey, she smiled down at him, her dark eyes soft and tender.

"You can't help yourself, can you?" Her voice had a tiny quaver in it.

"Can't help myself what?"

"Being gentle. You're so caring; if my heart was breaking you'd fix it." She paused, "it's not breaking though."

Amanda suddenly put her finger to her lips, sshhh.

"What, what is it?" Adam whispered.

"Keep still... Oh yes, I can feel it, your cock inside me, its beat, fuck, it's delicious." She pulled her legs up on each side of his body, squeezing with her thighs. She sat up, and Adam saw a long flush of red on her throat and above her breasts. Amanda's cunt clenched his cock, and his eyes flickered closed. "Oh yes, you've not come yet, have you, lovely man? I wonder... Don't you move," she warned, "not until I say."

Still impaled on his shaft, Amanda lay down beside him, and he cradled her smallness in his arms. Facing each other, they slowly began to move together. Amanda had come once, fiercely, but now she would make him rise and rise and rise into her. "Ah ah ah, don't you move," she said, "it's my turn now. I'm going to make you come. When I'm good and ready."

Amanda clenched down onto his cock, and began to slowly slide, up, down, up. Adam lay still, his only movement the beat of his cock with his heart; and his hand, swirling slow circles with his fingers up and down her spine, up and down. They were so slow together, so slow.

Bliss built, slow ecstasy, sliding, sliding, her slow fuck onto his length. She was still heated from her earlier orgasm, and the thick heat of his big cock in her tight cunt was pressing against her clit on one stroke, then full inside her on another.

Amanda gasped, "Do you want me, want me, Adam?" Her dark eyes flickering open and shut with her pleasure. "Your honey child, your sweetest thing?" She clenched onto his cock. "Move with me, Adam, my Adam." She used his name like a metronome, moving long on his shaft now, fucking him with her sweet wetness, her wet sweetness. "Do you like your coffee girl, Adam, your little coffee queen, fuck me, fuck yes, into me, Adam, me, just me..."

Their movement together surrendered them up to each other, and Amanda found her voice, and they fucked to her words. "What, sir, will it be?" Shafting thickness, open wetness, "one sugar or two sugar, sir?" Fucking into each other, grappling hands. "Latte or black sir, Jesus, fuck, your cock, oh yes, into me, harder, fuck, harder. Oh Adam, are you nearly there, nearly there, fuck me, yes, fuck, in my cunt, in my wet pussy, show me what those women taught you, Adam, Adam..."

Adam rolled so he was over her, Amanda's body under him on the bed. He fucked long strokes into her, his whole shaft pulling back so the tip of his cock almost left her sex with each stroke, then back into her long and deep. Amanda stuttered words, incoherently now, and was silent, her mouth open and her eyes wider with each stroke, his cock, cock, thick full, deep wet, fuck, cock, cunt, fucking her so full, with his gentleness in every stroke. She didn't want him hard and furious, she craved his length and slowness, every moment of their fuck was longer, tantalising her, building her back up to another peak.

Her eyelids flickered closed, red shining, then blue and crackling white as colours intensified in her mind. Her legs were wrapped around his hips and she was so open to this man, the slick of her sex so smooth as he stroked. Her hands gripped his ass, pulling her, pulling her into him, deeper. She was small beneath him but her cunt was all around him as she made him hers.

"Adam, fuck, fuck me, your cock, my cock, mine, fuck, mine, give it to me, I want it, me, me, fuck, yes, cunt, my cunt, fill my cunt, hard, hard, now, oh God, o uhh, ohhh," Amanda's words turn into formless sounds, and he spoke to her, echoing her peaking climb.

"Lovely girl, my love, my love, fuck, sweet you I'm fucking you, little honey, yes, oh fuck, yes, yes, oh h Mandy, my Amanda, Mandy in the morning, oh fuck, my honey, here I'm, fuck, ohhh..."

His long body tightened above her, his cock deep, so deep inside her. Her hands pulled him a fraction deeper, and their movement stopped. All movement stopped in the room except their fast beating hearts, and with three long throbs, then four, Adam came inside her. Amanda felt only his throb inside her. Adam's pulsing cream filled her, and her orgasm shuddered up through her body, triggered by the sensation of his pulsing inside her. She uttered a low moan and with a final upwards thrust of her sex, "Oh h my sweet fuck, oh h uhh," she was bliss.

She rolled beside him and he followed her, still inside, filling her. Adam wrapped her delicate body in his arms. She gripped him, not letting him go, and they were together, side by side. Lovers in a loving place, she held him, her sex like a kind hand as he softened. "Oh Adam, don't go," she whispered, and he stayed.

Sometime in the night Amanda woke to find him spooning her, his knees up cradling her bottom, his hand cupping a breast, and his other hand outstretched on the bed, his forearm a pillow for her cheek. His breath was deep and steady, a little catch in his throat, sometimes. She reached for her phone on the table beside the bed, two missed calls. She checked the time, two twenty.

Tomorrow was Friday, she had to be at work, early. But she was in town already, which meant an hour and a bit extra. She remembered his words, I'm still warm in my bed, and smiled. Warm in his bed, yes.

Goodness. She vaguely wondered what she was doing, and knew she must call Ant in the morning. She nestled her bum down against the warmth of Adam's groin, feeling his coiled heat behind her. Within minutes she was asleep, cradled and small and safe in his bed.

In the morning Amanda dressed as he watched her. She was efficient and practical, putting her long hair up into its ponytail, smoothing her skirt down over her hips, pencil on her eye lids, Cleopatra. She paused, looked down at herself, and reached up under her skirt to remove her knickers and gave them to him. "The cloth clings to my curves much tighter, don't you think, without the underwear?"

"Yes, I do like it," Adam replied, thinking he might buy her a garter belt to hold up fine stockings, rather than her plain hose. The thin lines of garter straps under a tight skirt were always enticing.

"I'll have breakfast at the café, like I always do," she said, her morning routine replacing night together. "Adam..." she went to the bed, leaned down and kissed him. "Thank you. Thank you so much for yesterday, and last night. It was wonderful. You spoil me."

"Amanda, I'm the one who must thank you. You're young, so fresh, I'm the lucky one."

"Both of us, then, lucky and spoiled." She kissed him again, and ran her fingers over the grey stubble on his jaw. "You need a shave.

"Good morning, Adam, your usual?"

"Yes please, Amanda, my usual." He passed her the correct change, just as he always did.

"Your money's always warm," she said. "Other people give me change from a purse, and it's cold in my hand."

"Oh well, you know what they say. Warm hands, cold heart," Adam replied.

"Oh no," Amanda said, "I don't think you're that kind of a man at all, not at all." Her fingers just grazed his, and lingered. "Not cold at all."

The Blue Silk Dress

"So who is he, Amanda?"

"He's just a customer at the café. I sell him coffee in the mornings. We chat, when there's no queue."

"You must do more than chat, if he gives you this."

"This" was a wrapped box Amanda brought home from the café that day. It sat unopened on the table between her and Antony. In every way, it sat between Antony and Amanda; her boy not knowing what it meant, Amanda knowing exactly what it meant.

Adam had given Amanda the choice when he placed the box on the counter that morning. She chose to take the gift home knowing that Antony would eventually see it, and like Scarlett in the morning she would have to cope with whatever reaction he had. At least, she hoped there would be some kind of a reaction from Ant, to show that he cared.

"What is it? What does it mean?" Antony didn't know. He was scared to know.

"I don't know what it is, but it will be beautiful, I'm sure." Adam doesn't do plain, she thought, remembering her afternoon with him at the fashion exhibition. Whatever it is, it will be wonderful. She assumed it was Adam's way of saying he wanted to be with her again. His confidence amazed her.

But then, she had astonished herself that evening as well, thoroughly enjoying the ebb and flow of their togetherness. One minute he took her somewhere sensual, decadent and luxurious, then it was her turn to take him. To take him, and to be taken. Oh god, she wanted that again. She clenched her thighs together, a heat spreading in her belly.

Amanda knew she was testing Ant, and knew she was unfair doing so. Sometimes she just wanted to shake him, slap him even, just to get him to react. In her way she loved the young man, but Adam set such a high bar now. She knew she was unfair to Ant. He was so out of his depth.

The spreading heat in her belly, and the knowledge that she could seduce Antony in a moment, gave her a new confidence. But I mustn't play with him, she thought, that would be cruel. She gazed at him, admiring his slim beauty.

She knew they made a good looking couple, with her elfin looks and Ant's lithe, blond grace, but he frustrated her so. His emotional distance drove her mad, sometimes. Just when she wanted him to stay, he would go, his mates calling and his games. His games, his constant, mind numbing games. Sometimes his fingers were more adept on his damned XBox controller than they were on her.

Now though, the idea of Adam and his worship in her head at the end of the day, she was horny, her mood shifting hot, and she would seduce her boy. She knew how to do that, slowly and with great delight.

Amanda reached for Ant's face, her fingers gentle from learning Adam's touch and understanding his slowness. "It's OK, Antony, I can handle it."

Antony winced away from her touch, and Amanda's eyes darkened, her mercury rising for a fight. A thread of adrenaline pulsed into her cunt, her nipples tightened and her fingers gripped the wood of the table. She waited for Ant's next move. Adam's parcel was a challenge between them, and her heat Antony's reward, if he could find it.

"But what the fuck is it, this fucking box wrapped so nice?" Antony's anger was rising, but he was beating on himself too. When was the last time he had given Amanda anything? He picked the box up from the table, but had the sense to open the parcel carefully and not tear the paper. He could see the care that had gone into the wrapping, and wondered about the man who would do that, care so much about little details. He looked at Amanda watching him, and thought he had never seen that look on her face before.

She watched his face as he turned the box over and removed its lid. Antony looked upon the contents, confusion on his face. He placed the box on the table, and his movement had a quiet reverence to it, for even he could recognise quality, especially when it was right in front of him. Amanda was right in front of him, but he didn't always see her. He glanced up, but not to her eyes.

"Why? Why is he sending you this? What have you done to deserve this?"

Amanda reached inside the box and took out the folded dress, a silver blue, silken blue dress. She stroked the surface of the cloth with her hand, a slow caress, and remembered Adam's caress of her skin, a gentle caress.

"Because it's beautiful," she replied, "it's because he likes beautiful things."

Antony looked at her. They were both standing, the table between them and the box and its silken contents between them even more, a gulf of understanding dividing them. Antony didn't understand at all. Amanda wanted him to, she wanted him to see her beauty when it was right before him.

"Are you fucking him, Amanda? This man, are you fucking him?"

Amanda looked at him, her eyes dark. "No, Ant, I'm not fucking him." He's too gentle for that. "You're the one who fucks me, then you leave me."

Her voice was steady, her passion controlled and directed towards him. She wasn't angry with her boy, she just wanted him to see that she craved love, wanted gentleness, his attention. She wanted him to see her, the girl right in front of him. Look at me, Ant, am I beautiful? Look at me.

He didn't see her, all he could see was the dress.

"You bitch, Amanda, you fucking bitch. Jesus, that's where you were that night, wasn't it? With him, fucking him."

Amanda didn't say a word. Instead, she slowly made her way around the table and stood right in front of Antony. He was quivering; she was in control now. She looked up at him, her dark eyes wide, her lips ever so slightly opened, her small teeth a promise of a nip and a bite. Amanda smiled. She reached down.

"Antony, are you jealous? Does the idea of someone else fucking me get you hard?" She gripped him. "Gets you hard now, doesn't it?" She squeezed his length, and his cock gave an answering throb.

She pushed him backwards, through the door and down the hall, through the door to her bedroom, gripping his iron hard cock held tight in his jeans, her fingers feeling its heat through the cloth. She slammed shut the door and pushed him up against it, her hand still firm on his prick. She had him, literally, in the palm of her hand.

"Oh Antony," she crooned, "you want me, don't you." It was a statement, not a question. She squeezed. "The thought of someone else fucking me, your Amanda. It gets you hot, doesn't it? You thought I was yours, didn't you?" She was relentless. She pressed her palm hard against his crotch, pushing his ass back against the door. "You're mine, now."

Amanda tilted her head up to his, and took his mouth with hers, her tongue fucking him, pressing between his lips, taking his mouth. Her hand on his hardness gripped, feeling the shape of his shaft, and it hurt, so hard in his jeans but trapped. With her other hand, she reached for the buttons of his shirt, undoing them one by one.

Antony's hands were helpless, hanging, he didn't know what to do in the face of her heat. Amanda pulled the cloth of his shirt aside, revealing his chest and a fine thread of dark hair down the centre and a crucifix to his nipples.

With her small sharp teeth she teased up one nipple, sucking and biting it into her mouth, and her cunt opened up and she was wet for him. The hand on his groin widened, her fingers spreading around his trapped, sideways shaft, and her fingers splayed and tightened, gripping and releasing.

Helpless moans fell from his mouth. "Fuck, Amanda, I..."

"Hush, Ant, it's OK, just do as you're told, be my boy." Amanda's voice was a low sing-song, her aroused huskiness a low, sweet threat, a promise. "Just let Amanda..."

She silenced herself with her mouth on his, and this time as she kissed him, both hands dropped to the buckle of his belt, and quick fingers undid the clasp. Antony pressed back against the door, his hands pushing back against the door jamb to steady himself, his head knocked back hard against the wood.

Amanda dropped down, her short skirt riding high on her thighs as she crouched before him. Her sex lips were opening wide, her panties a dark wetness hidden, the stretching of the cloth pulling tight against the crack of her ass. The wide crouch stretched the star of her asshole, and she was aware of her opening heat and the cooler air.

She crouched before him, and her skirt rode high. Both hands undid the buckle of his belt and the button of his jeans, and Amanda slid down the zip. The top of his jeans opened, and Amanda mouthed the line of dark hair descending down his centre into the darkness of his jeans. Antony was fair haired and smooth skinned, just fine trails of soft darkness on his chest and down the centre of his gut, and Amanda's tongue followed down the trail.

With one hand against his belly to hold him still, Amanda pushed his legs apart so he was steady, peeling down the tight skin of his jeans to his thighs, revealing the hard rod of his prick still sideways in his jockey shorts. She held her hand against him, not letting him straighten. She looked up to his face, his eyes were closed.

"Look, Antony, look at me."

He looked down and watched as Amanda extracted his rigid cock from his jocks, taking it in both her hands, her palms holding the heat of his shaft. Her fingers touched tips above its length, and the shape of her hands was the promise of her sex. She held him for a moment, his cock jutting from his groin. Then she pushed his shaft up against his gut and held it there with one hand, and with the other she pulled his jeans down so he stood naked before her.

She took his prick back in both her hands, and held him. His arousal was a beat, she held him. Amanda looked up to his face to make sure he obeyed her, was watching her, looking at her. Finally, she thought, he looks at me because I've got his cock in my hands. She thought of Adam's gaze, how he looked into her eyes and held her there. She remembered how she bent before Adam, displaying the firm curves of her ass and the small droop of her breasts, and smiled at the way she wrapped the curtains around herself.

Amanda closed her eyes, blocking out the memory of her older man, and turned her attention to the younger man thrust before her. She leaned forward, and with the most delicate motion, as if she were savouring a sweet ripe fruit, bite by bite, she opened her lips and took Ant's head into her mouth, slowly licking his end, piercing the small slit with her tongue. The feel of his hot cock head on her fingers, he was so hot and hard, was the same velvet touch of her own lips when she caressed herself. She slowly swirled her tongue over and around his swelling head, and he moaned.

"Fuck, Amanda, that's good, so sweet, suck me, oh fuck, fuck." Antony reached down with his hands, and held the back of her head. He started to thrust into her mouth. But Amanda pulled her head back, letting his cock fall from her hot lips.

"No Antony, you're not fucking my mouth. I'm sucking your cock." She pressed her hand against his belly, pressing him back against the wall. "You're not to move, it's my cock now, not yours."

Amanda returned to the shaft before her, and this time she kissed and licked the length of it, feasting her eyes on his beautiful cock, kissing it up and down with a quiet reverence.

"See Ant," Amanda's words were dreamy and slow, "you don't have to rush all the time. Your cock," and she twisted her hands around his head and pulled a sharp wince of pleasure from Ant's throat, "your cock is in no hurry. We've got plenty of time. So hot, it's so hot."

Again Antony reached his hands down to her head, but this time he stroked her hair gently, carefully. Amanda shook her head slowly, and her long hair swayed and caught on his arms, like a fall of soft rain. "See Ant, it's best slow, so slow."

Amanda sucked his head into her mouth, her tongue swirling under and over the most sensitive places. She allowed him to push into her mouth, pulling back when he thrust too deep, showing him her rhythm, sucking his cock, sucking his cock.

Her mouth grew wetter and she was hungry for him, her spittle looping long strings of glistening wetness when she pulled back for breath. Amanda sucked harder, her mouth slopping from his wet prick and grappling it into her mouth, deeper. Her cheeks sucked in, and his cock head thickened.

Antony's moans and cries grew louder, incoherent words shuddering from his mouth, and his hands left Amanda's hair. With a finger and thumb he pulled on his own nipples, alternating left and right, pinching his tight buds into rigid tips. Flicking fast with his finger tip, Ant teased pleasure into his nipples, like darts of ice behind his chest.

Amanda stretched one hand around his shaft, stroking, stroking, sucking in the head of him to her wet mouth, stroking. With her other hand Amanda reached into her own panties, pushing the wet cloth into her cunt, pulling the edge of the cloth tight against her heated asshole, sliding her fingers into her slippery wetness. She darted her fingers into her cunt, and put them up to Ant's mouth. He sucked hungrily on her taste and his cock thrust in response.

"Fuck me, faster Amanda, don't stop, oh h, fuck, my cock. Jesus, I'm getting close. I'm going to come, ahh, god, yes, fuck, in your mouth, Mandy, take me in your mouth."

Amanda kept up the steady stroke on his shaft, urging up his cream. Her mouth was wet with her spit and her lips were swollen and red around Ant's head. She sensed his closeness, and slowed her stroke, slowing him. Her hand went to grip his high balls, riding tight up against his body, and he shuddered. Amanda stopped her stroke, and his cock was rigid and tight. She looked up at him, his head knocked back, his fingers hopelessly gripping the wall behind him.

Beyond thought now, Ant barely registered the cooling air between his legs as Amanda bumped one foot wider, exposing his high, hot balls and his puckered asshole. Amanda slicked a wet mess of cunt juice and spit onto her forefinger, and probed it up into his hottest hole, pressing upwards relentlessly until her knuckle found the first tight ring of muscle. She eased back, and sucked his head deep into her mouth. Her finger pushed and pushed, then eased back again, working into him.

Deeper this time, and with a sobbing gasp, Ant accepted her finger's entry and his asshole took her.

With a suck on Ant's cock and a deep fingering, Amanda started a relentless probing finger fuck up his ass, and Ant's moans turned into sighs, "yes, yes, yes, fuck me Amanda, my ass, suck me, fuck, oh fuck yes, I'm going ..."

His semen was faster than his words, Amanda's finger fucking up inside him, and his cock erupted creamy fluid, spurting jets into her mouth.

Amanda drank his thrusts down as much as she could, but he was young and his balls were full, and his cum spilled and dripped down her chin. Amanda licked her tongue around his gorgeous mess, and smeared her chin with Ant's cream, loving it on her face, rubbing it into her skin.

Staggering backwards onto her bed, Amanda pulled her naked man on top of her, Ant's softening cock shining with his cum and her spit. Cum still dripped from his cock, and smeared a trail on her skirt and over her thigh. She loved the smell of him, the sweet odour of his jism ripe in her room, and underneath the rich smell of her own arousal.

She loved that she was dressed and Ant was naked; somehow it meant he was hers now, naked and soft before her, her boy. Amanda wrapped her arms around Antony, stroking his fair hair and kissing him, softer now, more gentle with him than before. She was making him stay with her, her dishevelled clothes a promise, because of course he must undress her and cradle her in his arms, make love to her later.

"Antony," her voice was soft with her love for him, "you mustn't be jealous, not anymore." Amanda touched her fingers to his cheek, claiming Ant for herself. "I'm not leaving you." She rolled onto her side, holding him. She pulled covers up around his naked body. "You mustn't get cold."

"Adam's a thing, I admit it. He's a fascination, and I like him. But he's... I don't know how to explain. But he's not you. Do you get that? He's not you."

Antony understood Amanda well enough not to push her. She was confessing something, but he didn't know what.

"But the dress. What does the dress mean?"

"It's nothing. It's just a dress. Adam likes beautiful things, but it's just a dress."

At the Private Function

Adam arrived at the gallery just after six. He greeted the owners and was introduced to the young artist showing her first exhibition. Never good at small talk, he took his wine glass and moved slowly around the walls, studying each painting, each small drawing. From time to time he would stop, fascinated by a small detail here or a particular spray of colour there. He kept half an eye on the door. He didn't know when Amanda would arrive, but was sure she would.

The gallery filled and Adam found himself caught up in conversations he didn't really want to have, with people he didn't really care for. In the crowded room he gave up watching the door, and waited instead for a shift in the sound of the room, a lull of silence as heads turned and the air held its breath.

Adam turned, and there she was. Amanda made a quiet entry into the room, a slim figure in the vintage silk, silvery blue dress. Her hair was coiled high in a tight twist on her head, accentuating her elegant neck. Instead of the usual diamond studs in her ears, Amanda wore a pair of perfectly dropped pearl earrings. The dress was a vintage fifties design, a strapless sweetheart bodice fitted tight to Amanda's delicate waist, swirling wide over her hips. It was the type of dress that could only be worn by a girl of a particular, perfect age.

Adam gazed at her and Amanda was everything he wanted her to be. He watched as Amanda was approached by a waiter, and it was only right that she should be served, this little coffee girl going out in the evening. She took a cocktail glass from the waiter's tray, and the colour of the drink, the palest blue, matched her dress. The waiter said something and Amanda laughed. She touched the waiter's hand on the tray in a greeting or a conspiracy, just as she had touched Adam's arm one long ago lunchtime. I called her honey, thought Adam, and she smiled at me.

He smiled to himself, and the woman beside him turned and asked, "daydreams, or sweet dreams?" Adam was gracious and charmed her for a moment. The woman sensed his distance and touched his arm to remember, but knew without a word she was not tonight, not with him.

"Josephine, is that you, where have you been hiding?" Adam was rescued by the gallery owner, who had given Adam two tickets and knew he was waiting for someone else. Josephine looked back at Adam, an ache in her belly and a longing to be longed for by him.

Amanda mingled through the crowd, slowly making her way to Adam. He stood waiting, and Amanda came up to him and kissed his cheek. "Adam. Thank you, this is wonderful, thank you so much for the invitation." Her discretion was perfection, but her eyes shone just for him in that moment. Adam's heart stopped and started, and he remembered to breath.

She stretched up to whisper in his ear, "have you got..."

"Yes, on the 22nd floor this time, higher up than before."

"Oh goodie, I can pretend it's my birthday floor." She quickly gripped his fingers, and her hand reminded him of mornings at the café.

Oh goodie? Adam marvelled at the girl. Amanda sometimes forgot she was a young woman, dropping years off her age.

"When will we leave? There are people I want to meet first."

Amanda's eyes were bright with her excitement for later, but also wide with her love of people, now. She thrived on the whirl of conversation and movement, and was like a rippling stream high in the mountain. Adam was the opposite, a still rock who preferred the water to flow around him. Crowds exhausted him, and his energy came from the only one before him.

Amanda was fuelled by movement. "I'll be back, don't worry."

Adam didn't worry. He smiled at her back as she flitted into the room, watching her swirl within the crowd. She was a natural at it, and charmed people in her silvery blue silken dress.

Adam sipped from his glass, stepping forward to read a label describing the painter's approach to the work in front of him. As he slowly moved back, he became aware of a presence beside him, so close. Before he could speak, the young man beside him turned away, looking across the room, nervous agitation in his tapping fingers. Adam followed his gaze, and there was Amanda circled by several men, hipsters and cool.

Ah, thought Adam, I see. He waited for the boy to turn back. "You must be Antony. Hello, I'm Adam."

"Yes, hello. How did you know?"

"Oh, Amanda's talked about you. She adores you." Adam knew he had to charm Antony and flatter him. "You do know that, don't you?" He paused. "It's in her eyes when she says your name. Ant, that's right, isn't it? She loves you. Surely you know that?"

"What are you...? I mean, yes. Amanda..." Antony lost track of what he was trying to say. He was still confused as to who Adam was, and was surprised to find the other man older than he expected. He had conjured up images of meeting Adam, confronting him, this other man getting between him and Amanda. But the last thing he expected to hear was that Amanda adored him, loved him. "What? Wait. Amanda said that?"

"No. She hasn't said anything about love. She doesn't need to. It's in her eyes whenever she mentions your name." Adam looked around. Amanda had seen the two of them together, and was making her way to her men. Antony saw Adam looking away, and turned his head to see.

"God, that's a beautiful dress." Ant couldn't help himself, he had to say something.

"No," Adam said. "Amanda's a beautiful girl wearing a dress. It's just a dress, Antony, just a dress." He stopped talking, because he knew damn well it wasn't just a dress.

"Ant. What are you doing here?" Amanda was between the two men, instinctively separating them. "How did you get in?"

"I know the guy on the door."

"Oh. OK. You've met Adam, then."

"No, not really. He knows me, but I don't know who he is." Adam heard the tension in Antony's voice and wondered if the young man was aching for a fight. He wondered if Ant knew that Amanda had spent a night with him.

"I told you," replied Amanda, "Adam buys coffee in the mornings, and we went to the Gallery to see that Tate exhibition." She paused. "The one you didn't want to go see."

"But I..."

"Not now, Antony. You didn't want to see it. Adam did, he was going anyway, and we bumped into each other outside the café. So he took me."

Adam wondered if Antony heard her double meaning. He looked at the boy, and wondered if Antony was hearing anything at all.

Amanda stood between them. Adam remained silent, impressed by the girl's control, waiting for her next move. She looked at both men, so different, both hers at that moment.

Amanda decided.

"Adam, can we go now, please?"

She turned to her younger man, and Adam saw her eyes soften at the sight of his lost, confused look.

"Antony, I want you. Tonight and tomorrow, and the day after that, I want you." Amanda wasn't a cruel girl, but she was determined. "But I'm not yours, not ever, for you to decide what I do." She took Antony's hand in hers, and he didn't pull away, not this time.

"But tonight, you're both mine."

Amanda walked between them down the hallway. In the base of her belly her cunt was blooming, aching to be filled. She was wet already, her heart pounding with heightened expectation. Amanda knew that Antony would be fast and impatient, his youth and misunderstanding getting in the way, his heat and energy untamed. Ant didn't know how to seduce her, either slowly or fast. He was unformed and beautifully careless.

She knew, too, that Adam would be slower, patient, far more deliberate. He would tease and tantalise her higher and higher, so high she would soar. Adam would handle her with the greatest delight and care, a delicacy. He would be the one to reveal her from his dress.

Amanda had turned the shimmering blue cloth over in her hands before slipping it over her head, the silk a shivering cold on her skin, and saw the faint stain on its hem. It was a vintage original, delicate and faded in places where Amanda looked close. Her thank-you to Adam, his first delight, would be to reveal herself to him in the dress. Antony could watch (she would see his cock thicken and rise), but her eyes would be on Adam. He had chosen the dress for her. Amanda wondered who wore it first, when it was new.

Amanda also knew that Antony was still uncertain of her motives. She remembered his powerful sexual response earlier in the week, so aroused at the idea of her with someone else. She didn't care if it was jealousy or an alpha male thing to prove himself, all she saw was his arousal and uncontrolled explosion of lust. That was enough. A response from him, on her terms; enough for the time being, at least. A sweet fuck, Ant was her boy.

Even though Adam was still and brooding, a darkness in him sometimes with his long, unknown and silent past, somehow Amanda felt on safer grounds with Adam. She had discovered that Adam was a Leo, and the star sign suited his nature. She could safely play with him like a little cub plays between a lion's paws, her little teeth and claws sharp, but all the while cradled safe. Even in his darker places, Amanda knew she was Adam's girl and always safe.

Amanda wondered how she would be, spun between their molten mercury and liquid gold, her own incandescent silver threading them all around. Alchemy was in the air, magical threads shifting and mingling between them.

She smiled at her thoughts. More truly I'm like a young lioness in heat, rolling on my back before him, my legs spread and my belly exposed.

Now though, Amanda was beautiful in her lovely dress, and two men to do with as she desired; one because he loved her, the other because he indulged her.

In an Upstairs Room

Shutting the door with a solid click, Amanda spun before Adam and Antony, a pirouette on a high toe. She kissed their lips with her finger tips, and darted to a seat by the window. She saw her reflection in the glass, and reached to the back of her head, unpinning her hair and it fell like a fall of silk past her shoulders, a long twist to her waist. Amanda leaned back in the chair, and her eyes were wide and black.

"So," she said, her voice husky with her own lust, "why are you both dressed?"

Antony stumbled at her command, and bent down to pull off his shoes, standing to pull the shirt from his jeans. Amanda smiled at his eagerness, his desire to please her. She could see already the shape of him, angled down. A thread tightened around her clitoris, pulling a tight stab of pleasure upwards. She shifted in the chair, her thighs widening just a little, her lips reddening with heat between her legs.

"Slowly," she heard Adam's low voice. "Tease her. Make her wait."

You beautiful bad man, she thought, you always know what to do, know what I want

"Adam," she asked, "what colour was your hair, when you were young like Antony?"

"Like Antony?" Adam wondered. "When I was twenty-two, twenty-three?" He looked at Ant's fair hair, cut short. "At that age, it was going darker already. I liked it best when I was twenty, it was long and blond, a golden blond in the sun." Amanda loved his crooked smile as he remembered himself. "I was a blond golden boy in summer, tanned and bleached from days by the pool, by the sea."

Goodness, the girls must have loved you, a blond poetry boy, your head in the clouds.

"Was there an Anna, back then?" Amanda remembered his first guess at her name, back in the café. You look like an Anna.

"Anna? No, there's never been an Anna, not for me." He smiled at her, understanding now. "Oh, I see. No, you didn't remind me of someone else. Just the name, it would suit you. I don't know why." Even as he was speaking, Amanda watched him slowly undo the buttons on his shirt.

"Turn around, away from her," she heard Adam say. He turned, taking his hands away from her sight.

"What? Oh..." Antony, keep up, she thought. And he did. She gazed at their backs, these two men undressing before her. She admired the tight curve of Antony's firm, hard ass, muscles taut and tight from his soccer. He was slimmer than Adam, not so tall, and his young fit body was firmer, harder.

Oh fuck, thought Amanda, I want to press myself against your back, reach around and feel the heat of your cock, undo your belt. She shivered as Ant's hands disappeared in front of him, where she could not see. He was undoing his belt, and she saw a long strap of leather in his hand as he pulled it from its buckle.

A quick image flashed across Amanda's mind: her wrists strapped with that belt, her hands behind her back, kneeling on the carpet...

With one swift movement Adam pulled his trousers down, his underwear at the same time, to reveal his long legs. His body was thicker than Ant's, broader across the shoulders, but softer. He was his age, but wore it well.

Like he always did, Antony pulled his jeans down first, hopping from one leg to the other to peal the tight cloth away. He always left his briefs on for a moment, and was strangely shy, turning away from her look to pull them off. Now, he was already facing away, but was still strangely shy. Amanda could see from the tilt of his head that he glanced down towards Adam, and wondered if he saw the older man's thicker cock hanging down.

Adam leaned in towards Antony, whispering something in his ear. Amanda saw the boy flinch away, Adam whispering still, and Ant's body lost some of its tension. Amanda wondered what Adam had said.

Whatever it was, Ant was happier. They stood motionless, their backs to Amanda.

She shifted in the chair, leaning back into the cushions, her thighs creeping apart. Her nipples tightened and she watched the tableau unfold. Adam was a showman, and she was learning the delight of her gaze.

Antony leaned over and pulled the briefs down his legs. Amanda loved his taut ass, and would grip those cheeks with her hands as she pulled him into her, fucking in the morning, tight and hard.

Fuck, they were teasing her, she wanted them to turn slowly so she could see their cocks. But they didn't turn, they were denying her. Ant glanced over his shoulder, but Amanda didn't really see. She was feasting her eyes on his ass, waiting, waiting.

The girl knew that Adam was orchestrating everything for his own jaded pleasure and for Amanda's delight. She wasn't quite sure where Antony might fit into Adam's plans, but he didn't seem surprised that Ant was here. Maybe it was inevitable there would be a confrontation.

Oh my, thought Amanda, I wonder what Ant thinks about that? Adam had run his hand slowly down her boy's side and around to the base of Ant's belly. Oh fuuuck, Amanda sighed, as she figured out where Adam's hand had gone. Antony, you're hard already, Adam has your cock up against your gut, I can see from the angle of his arm. Antony confirmed the geometry of limbs and angles by the arch of his throat, his head thrown back in pleasure. Amanda whimpered, I want to see.

She sank back further into the soft chair, pulling the dress up high to reveal the tops of her thighs and white stockings. Amanda cupped her sex with the palm of her hand. Adam had admired the shape of her bare bum when she dressed before him in the morning, and she wore no knickers tonight. Her fingers dipped and she moaned.

Antony moaned, and Amanda stroked her clit hard. Ah fuck, Adam was on his knees in front of Antony, he must have her boy's cock in his hand, in his mouth. Amanda writhed. She saw Ant's feet shift wider, and oh bliss, there were Adam's fingers shifting over Ant's tight balls, curving up four fingers over one ass cheek. Amanda watched entranced as Antony shifted his weight up onto his toes, lifting his cock deeper into Adam's mouth, it must be deeper. His body dropped and Amanda knew, she just knew, that Ant had dropped his hot asshole down onto Adam's thumb.

Amanda and Antony often played with each other's asses, both enjoying the tight grip and musky taste, and here was Ant, opening his tight channel to Adam's thumb. Amanda shivered, dipping her fingers into her hot wetness, pressing hard against her clit. Oh sweet fuck, she might get Ant to lick out her ass tonight. He didn't do it often, but sweet goodness, Amanda loved the dark taboo of his tongue and fingers there.

Adam, she thought, does Adam like ass too? She'd never thought of that before. Adam spoke about learning from his women. Did he have some musky darkness in his past he might want again? Men and women? She didn't know.

Amanda's mind raced with the thought of hot cock and tight holes. She thought of different combinations. Oh my, I think I'll be sore by the time I'm done with two cocks tonight. Her fingers dipped deeper. Amanda heard Ant's moan, she heard him moan for Adam, "More."

Adam had the shaft of the young man's rigid, hot cock in his hand and the red heart shaped end of it in his mouth, his tongue swirling, sucking. This was his first cock for a long, long time and Adam took his time with it. Closing his eyes, Adam's senses focused on taste and heat and the hot flesh filling his mouth.

"More," Ant moaned again, and his hands went to the back of Adam's head, holding his sucking mouth onto the rock hard prick. Adam bumped Antony's thighs apart, then snaked his hand, his spit wet thumb, over Ant's tight balls to cup his tight ass. Adam delicately placed the pad of his thumb on the younger man's hole to entice and tease him. Adam felt Antony rise and fall, his weight opening his fierce hot place onto Adam's thumb, and Ant succumbed to the pleasure.

Adam had Amanda's boy pinned in a delicate place, and he marvelled at the speed the boy's anger had turned to shameless gratification. Adam thrust his thumb up deeper, a short hard fuck into Ant's ass, but this night was for Amanda, so the fuck was short and sweet. Antony gripped Adam's thumb and tried to hold him, but Adam's will was stronger and he pulled away, emptying Ant's hole. Adam stood, his fingers still around Ant's heated cock, his breath on the boy's neck.

"Kiss me," he whispered, "and we'll turn to Amanda." He paused, and gripped Antony's prick. "She wants to see, it's her turn now."

Adam pressed his bigger body up against the youth's finer frame, and kissed Antony hard on his lips, fucking his mouth, taking him with his tongue. Antony tongue fucked him back, and their hands trailed down to their asses. "Turn sideways so she can see."

With a slow turn (Ant was beginning to understand the slowness of time now) they moved so Amanda could see. And they saw her. Amanda had abandoned herself to the visual pleasure of the men together in the room. She sprawled in the chair, one leg resting on the arm to widen her sex, the other straight out before her. Her fingers dipped, and she tasted herself.

Adam's cock was thick and long, and throbbed as he saw the girl. Ant's cock was slender and smooth, but Adam liked cunt so much more, he always had. Tonight, though, was Amanda's fantasy made real, seeing two men with hard cocks before her eyes. "Press them together, your cocks, let me see."

She knew Ant's cock well, its slim inches sliding between her fingers, slipping into her sex, spurting cream on her breasts when she was too tired to take him. She remembered Adam's longer shaft from their evening together and wanted to compare shafts and thicknesses, longer inches, deeper thrusts.

"Show me now, please, please show me," she begged.

The men moved close to her chair and stood so that Amanda could see and touch them, right before her eyes, and take them into her hands. Her fingers were pussy wet, and she anointed the wonderful, beautiful pricks before her.

"Lovely," she murmured, "your cocks are so lovely." Amanda crouched forward in her chair. "Come here," she whispered, "let me feel you on my cheeks. So soft, oh god, the skin is so soft. Soft and hot."

Both men looked down at the girl, her face veiled behind her hair. She took one cock in her hands, both hands, and it was Antony's heat she took. She kissed the head of his cock and held it to her cheek. She knelt before them, and took the other shaft into a hand, and it was Adam's. She held his shaft against her cheek, thick and hard, her fingers a long, slow caress.

"So beautiful, so hot. Adam and Antony, Antony and Adam." She kissed and licked each prick in turn to her sing song song, and her cunt wept with the love of them. "Will you fuck me now, Adam? I want your long cock to fill me, fill my cunt." She stroked and caressed Antony's cock. "And my ass, Antony, you in my ass, oh fuck I'll be filled with you both." Her voice was slow and dreamy, as if in her mind she was already there, between them, fucked by the two of them.

"I'm in your dress, Adam, I need to get out of the dress." Amanda was nearly delirious with the idea of them both inside her. "Help me out of the dress."

Antony stood back and watched, knowing that the dress had some meaning to Adam, even though the older man insisted, it's just a dress. Ant thought it was some ceremonial thing, a special revelation of a beautiful girl within a beautiful dress. Adam had the honour of slipping it off Amanda's slender body. Antony watched, and finally understood that the girl was beautiful and he should tell her so. He never did. She was proud, he'd not fully seen that before, he'd never really seen her. Antony gazed upon Amanda with new eyes.

Her eyes were closed, she was languid, almost in a swoon.

Antony looked at Adam, and saw how he gazed at the girl with fondness, and something else Ant couldn't place. Perhaps a memory, or maybe a memory being made. Or a memory lost.

Adam leaned over Amanda, helping her to her feet, his hands at her waist. Amanda slowly placed her arms around his neck and turned up her face, not for a kiss but to rest her cheek on Adam's shoulder. He held her delicate grace in his arms.

"Dance with me, Adam, dance with me in your arms." Amanda's eyes were still closed and she clung to him.

They moved slowly around the room, silently dancing, one turn and another. They danced for a moment, a memory; they danced to forget, a slow pirouette. Amanda's heart ached for this man who held her, and the depths of her belly, too. They stopped by the bed, and Adam carefully slid down the zip at the back of the dress, down to her waist.

Antony, sitting on the bed now, saw that Amanda's back was bare, bra-less. Adam slowly ran his hands up and down the nubs of her spine, and she shivered. His hands were feather light on her skin, so soft, so gentle. He moved his palms up her sides, tenderly sliding the cloth from Amanda's arms so that her upper body was covered still by the dress, her small breasts cupped by the bodice.

With a swift move of the cloth, Amanda's torso was bared, those tight nipples exposed. Her breasts were a delight for Adam when he looked down. He leaned in to her mouth and kissed her. She was hungry in return and her tongue pushed. Adam thickened against the warm silk of the dress and Amanda felt his heat against her.

On the bed, Antony stroked his cock slowly, staring at Amanda's breasts pulled tight by her nipples. Her skin was dusky, some gypsy in her blood, and her breasts were firm and small. Her nipples, her hard tips Antony knew so well in his mouth, were tight and dark and he loved her.

Amanda opened her eyes, as if she could feel the pull of Antony's gaze, and saw his look. Her heart melted, he looks at me, finally, like Adam looks at me. She smiled and her eyes softened. They both adore me. She bathed in it like Cleopatra in her milk.

Impatient to be out of the dress, to be naked before them, Amanda shimmied it from her hips, and the blue silk fell in a crumpled pile to the floor. She stepped from it and was glorious in a pair of white stockings and a fine white garter belt.

"Ah sweetness," Adam said, "you're a pretty girl tonight. Antony, don't you think so?"

"She's always beautiful." Ant looked at the girl before him, standing confident in her nudity. "Amanda, I don't say it enough, do I? I think it, but I don't say it."

"It's OK Ant. I know you think it. But you do drive me nuts sometimes, your silence. It's why I love Adam so, it just comes naturally to him to show affection, he makes it seem easy."

Adam supported the boy. "It took me years to figure it out, Ant, what pleases a woman. I'm still figuring it out. Amanda here, she taught me a thing or two." He laughed. "But I think I taught her something as well. One day she'll tell me what it is. Women, Ant, they're impossible to follow."

"Umm, you two, I'm actually here in the room, you know." Amanda's eyes sparkled, she loved Adam's gentle teasing. "Shall I, you know, order beers or something?" She adored them both. "You sound like you're down the pub."

"Ah, no. Not the pub. A boudoir, maybe, a bordello. You can play the gypsy girl." Adam caught her by the waist and pulled her close. His heat pressed against her hip. "Caught between two lovers."

He signalled Ant to join them, and the two men pressed the girl between them.

"Close your eyes, Amanda my love. Close your eyes."

Amanda quivered at their touch, surrendering to their slow caresses. Her eyes closed and her sensations heightened. She tasted the air with her tongue, inhaling the rising scent of their hard, hot cocks. The slight musky tang of hot male heat was in the air, and beneath it the sweeter scent of her sex, her fingers dipped and on their lips in a promise.

Oh god, the sensation of four hands on her skin! Two hands she could follow, but the sensation of four hands overwhelmed her. Adam and Antony moved around her, their bodies grazing hers, pressing their hard heat up against her flesh. After some minutes she could no longer tell whose hands belonged to which man. They orchestrated different touches all around her, one moment feather light traces over her ass, then a firmer touch on her ribs. Adam ran his fingers through her hair, Antony ran two fingers along the slide of her lips and over her clitoris.

Oh sweet goodness, now Ant was in front of her. Amanda knew his familiar touch and the heat of his slender cock against her belly. His fingers tugged and teased her breasts, gentle and slow. She had shown him how to be gentle when they first met, but he was always so quick, a moment here and a moment there, then off somewhere else, too soon.

But now Ant was matching the movement of his hands to Adam's, who was the master of slow tease, tantalising her flesh as he traced patterns on her skin. Slowly, oh goodness, so very slowly.

Adam's bigger hands were on her waist and running up her back. He held her like a fine instrument, delicate and precious, made for a craftsman like him. The hot length of him was rigid heat against her back, and his heat soaked into her. "Oh my god, Adam, you play my body like a violin, such an exquisite song with your fingers."

He cradled her small rounded belly in one hand, cupping the outside of her womb in the palm of his hand. Amanda tilted her head back against his shoulder, and Adam's other hand went to her throat, the kindest restraint she had ever known.

Held still in his hands, Adam's belly and chest strong and tall behind her, Amanda was in her safest place. Held in his embrace, but always free to go whenever she wanted to go, Amanda stayed. In Adam's hands, she stayed.

Antony knelt before her, his hands gently parting Amanda's legs so that he could kiss and tongue her swollen, heated lips, covering the whole of her sex with his mouth. She was his chalice, his holy grail. Antony knelt before her and heard her sigh. "Oh, my Galahad, my lovely golden boy." He swirled her clit with his tongue, and she shivered. Ant parted her heated lips with honey dew on his fingers, and licked her again. She quivered.

"Amanda, where do you want us?" Antony was learning quickly. This was her thing, not his.

"Adam, in me, oh god, fill me with your length, stuff me hard. On your back, but in me so deep." Amanda was hungry for him, memories of their first night flashing in and out of her mind. He calls me honey and my love. Oh fuck. "Adam, please..."

"On the bed then, let me sort out these pillows." Adam sprawled his long body on the bed, and the girl lay on top of him, high up so she could kiss him. Amanda kissed him in the lips; and sweet Christ, the bloom of her cunt was right on the tip of his shaft.

"Antony, watch us, watch us close. See my cunt swallow Adam's cock." Amanda knew her boy loved words, filthy and seductive, sexy and strong, her woman's words. "See him fill me, oh fuck he fills me. My sweet, lovely cunt, see how I take him. Oh h fuck, Adam, you're so big, fill me, fill me, sweet Jesus, deeper. Fuck me."

Amanda started a low, shuddering commentary, her eyes dreamily shut. "Oh look, look, look at us. He's so big, so perfectly long for my tight cunt. But Ant, he's too big for me where I want you. In my ass Ant, my darkest tightest place. Remember our first time, Ant? In my ass. Fuck. Both my men.

"Hold his cock, Ant. Feel Adam as he slides into me, deep oh God deeper, Adam, fuck me, fuck me slowly. Fuck, oh, shit, fuck, fuck c k ooohh..."

Amanda eased herself down onto Adam's beautiful length, inch by wonderful inch, her sensation peaked by Ant's fingers stroking and swirling, slicking her juice over Adam's long shaft for lubrication. With a long, keening sigh she was on him, filled and impaled. Adam took her face in his hands and gazed deep into her big, black eyes, pupils dark with lust, dilated with desire.

Amanda squirmed on him, craving his cock thicker and deeper. Her insides opened up, oh sweet goodness, he was in her so deep. Amanda melted, her insides warm and wet. Adam's cock impaled her, oh fuck, she took him in, so much. Her belly ached with his long heat inside.

She stroked his adored face with one hand, and wrapped the other under his neck to hug him close. "Adam... oh fuck me slowly, Adam, my Adam." Amanda moved on his cock, filling her cunt with his heat. "Can I be your girl?"

They fucked slow and sweet, Amanda and Adam, their fingers entwined, her hair falling all over his face. Her small weight was on Adam's chest, the sweetest, smallest angel in the world. For a moment, time stopped and their movement was the only thing in the room, just them. A tiny moment, only for Adam, just for Amanda, a perfect little moment. Just the two of them. Count the seconds, then the time was gone.

"Antony, come to me, my darling boy. You too, I want you now."

Still languorously swaying on Adam's cock, Amanda widened her legs and there before Antony's eyes was the wrinkled puck of her asshole, a darker brown than her skin, a lovely twirl of flesh.

"You know what to do, Ant, open me up nice and slow with your fingers, push into me, that's right, slowly, slowly."

Amanda stopped her movement on Adam's shaft, concentrating on the new sensation. Antony's fingers in her tightest place were slow and insistent, but wait...

"Your tongue, Ant, fuck, yes, wet and hot, oh hh, mmmm." Her little pucker sucked at Ant's tongue as he pushed into that tight hole, spit on his mouth, wetting her for later. Amanda's ass tasted musky, earthy, a darker taste. Her sex juice was honey sweet, her ass like black coffee, a stronger taste.

"Am I wet, Ant? Quick, get some cream, slather your prick... Oh, that's it. Oooh, fuck me, fuuuucck me. Slowly, oh shit, you're big there... Oh, it hurts... not so, ooohh, yes yes mmmmm, uhh, ah ah ah."

Amanda panted as his cock eased into her, low growls from deep inside her body as she slowly took him in. Ant's slim body pressed down into her, entering her tight channel, his length the perfect length.

Adam began to kiss her, matching his breath into Amanda's mouth as she groaned with her lust and low anal pain. Their energy surged together, spiralling upwards with their breathing, and they began to rock together in a slowly moving, rhythmic pull and push.

Antony was deep in her now, stopping and pulling back a little to help her sphincter ease and open, then another push. Amanda moaned, quiet whimpers from her lips but she took Antony in, her beautiful man in her ass.

"Antony, yes, yes. Slowly, angel, move in me. Oh my god I'm stuffed so full. Fuck fuck fuck ooohh,"

Amanda took her weight onto her elbows, her fingers stretched out, gripping the sheets so she could push back onto Antony's probing cock. He was so deep into her ass now that his balls brushed the base of

Adam's shaft as the older man began to swathe his length into Amanda's slipping, wet pussy.

She was so wet that her juice creamed and frothed over both pricks, hot and lubricated, sliding sliding, the pace of the men still in rhythm, thrusting deeper into Amanda's helpless holes. She was pinioned between them, hot friction between the depths of her cunt and the tunnel of her ass. Each man could feel the heat and shift of the other man's shaft, sharing Amanda's openings.

She had never felt so much cock inside her. "Sweet god, I've never felt this good... I'm fucked, properly fucked, fuck me fuck me oh fuck me..." She didn't know which man she begged for most. "Now, harder, harder, Jesus, I'm going to come soon, don't ever stop. Ooohhh, fuck me hard, love me deep, my men, my lovely lovely men."

The two men set up a rhythm between them, Adam pushing the girl's body up with each stroke and Antony's weight shafting his cock deep into her ass. Inside her tight channels, Amanda felt the huge thickness of their cocks sliding against each other. She was split apart by their relentless thrusts, and a series of low moans and breathless sobs of pleasure sounded through the room.

"Yes, take me, take me, fuck me fuck me, faster, I want I want..." Amanda no longer knew what she wanted. Her body grew slippery with sweat as their thrusts impaled her, her cunt slick and wet; her ass hole wider as Antony slid in and out, spit and cream lubricating his swift fuck. Amanda was opening right up for him, sometimes even losing Ant's cock from her hole when he pulled back too far.

"In me, in me, come in my ass, come on fuck, I want your hot cream in me." Amanda sensed the heat in Antony's movements was different, faster. "Up my ass, come on, come in, come in me, me, oh god. In me, that's right fuck fuck come Ant come, harder baby, harder. I want you oh h fuck mmmm there there, oh Ant fuck, that's right, that's it ooohh, baby, baby spill it, oh god there, fuck fuck, hot cum, your hot cum. Your cock, spurting, cream me cream oh fuck. Come in my ass, baby, Antony..."

Amanda screamed his name as Antony pounded his cock into her ass, jetting his cum hot spurting deep up inside her.

"Mandy, fucking take it, my cock, take my cum. Oh fuck, I'm..."

Ant's orgasm jetted and pumped, his thick cum pulsed and pulsed inside her, jetting semen up her tightest channel. Ant was young, his prick was thick hard up inside her. Fucking up her ass, Antony shuddered his last surges deep inside Amanda.

"Mandy, oh fuck, Mandy, I love you, love your sweet ass."

The creamed slop of his cum slicked up her ass hole even more, and as Ant softened just a little, his strokes continued fast and deep. The sensation of his long shafting fuck touched Adam's cock, and he too started a faster climb to his own orgasm.

Somehow they all stayed in synch together, until Amanda began her milking of Adam's prick with her tight gripping sex and she too climbed and climbed, their orgasm hitting their bodies together, together, heated and fucked and coming together, Amanda and Adam fucked and fucked, coming so hard, and coming again.

"Ohhh fuck Amanda, take me all, take me, I'm coming..." Adam's thick cock shot his semen, his spurting cream, up into her tight cunt, and she gripped him, milking all of his hot, streaming seed from his balls.

Oh sweet fuck, Amanda came too and she gripped Adam's cock with her tight cunt as she spasmed, her mouth opened in a silent O. As she shivered, her muscles tightened around every channel, and in her ass Ant jetted his own final spurt.

Cum was everywhere, hot and rich, ribbons of white fluid, their movements turning it to a creamy froth as their shafting slowed and finally stopped. Panting filled the room as all three caught their breath.

"I'm fucked," mumbled Amanda, "I'm fucked and hot and sore. Doesn't matter, feels soooo good. Well and truly, properly, fucked."

She lay motionless, her body sprawled on top of Adam, her cunt and ass still filled with softening cocks and leaking cream. The smell of spunk and juice and sweat was hot in the room.

"Fucked, deliciously fucked and filled." Amanda was semi delirious with her shuddering pleasure, little aftershocks rippling through her. She languorously kissed Adam, biting his lip, sucking on his tongue.

"Oh Ant, my god, you filled me." She was full and aching in her ass with him, his cock felt huge. Ant had fucked so hard and fast and filled her with his strong young jets of cum. Her ass was hot and she felt an automatic push to expel him.

"Ohhh, don't go, oh uhh, nooo..." She cried out for Antony as his prick slid from her ass, and he fell sideways onto the bed. A hot pull of cum trailed wet from her hole down her thigh, dragged by his cock.

With Adam still inside her cunt, she pushed herself as far down onto his cock as she could, wanting him to stay. She wanted Adam to stay as long as he would, her payment for his love, his adoration of her. Amanda could have Antony whenever she wanted, but Adam was a rarer thing, a man who wanted her, just her, right now.

"I won't go, Adam. I'll fall asleep with you inside me and it will be the best dream ever." Amanda could only reach his throat to kiss him there. They rolled to their side with Adam's arms around her slender back, one hand stroking her lovely hair. Amanda cradled his face in her hands, gazing into his dark eyes looking back at her. Oh Adam, you looked at me and called me honey, your love.

Amanda felt Antony's body move up behind her, the long, sticky heat of him pressing between the cheeks of her ass, his thighs against the backs of hers. Ant's hand lay on her hip.

She was held in the safest of safe places, between the strong beating hearts of her men. As she closed her eyes and drifted, she felt Adam's arm move, and she knew his hand went around Ant's shoulder too, embracing both of them. Amanda smiled to herself. I've been fucked by two men who love me, she thought.

Oh Adam, you've been so wonderful for me and I'm proud to wear your dress, your beautiful dress. Antony, you silly boy, of course I love you, I think I always will. But you never bought me a lovely dress. Her mind lazily drifting between one man and two, Amanda slowly fell asleep like a falling leaf from a high tree. Her men held her, so small and beautiful, a precious girl so sweet.

Sometime in the night Amanda slid from Adam's cock, and rolled over to clutch her hands to Antony's chest, kissing him sleepily on the lips. She was aware of Adam's big warmth behind her, and nestled her ass back to his groin. She was safe with his solid strength behind her, he'd never let her fall.

In the morning, Adam woke first. He lay still, listening to their soft breathing. He eased himself from the bed and looked at the pair, their limbs intertwined. They were beautiful. Adam gazed upon them both before pulling up the covers of the bed to keep them warm.

They would wake later. Amanda would drowsily open her legs for Antony, and he would love her slowly, even if she was filled with another man's cum.

Adam picked the silvery blue, striped silken dress from the floor. He touched his finger to the small stain on the hem, a spill of wine he thought, from a party; and smiled as he saw another silvery stain higher up on the cloth. He put his nose to it, inhaling the faintest trace of Amanda. Another beautiful girl had left her mark. He carefully folded the dress and placed it in a carrier bag near his keys.

He left them a note, "Breakfast is on the room, all paid. Late checkout, but don't miss breakfast!"

Later, several months later, Adam received a post card in the mail, a rare thing nowadays.

"Send me a postcard," he had said, when she told him they were going, taking his money for coffee one last time. Amanda remembered, and bought a Japanese postcard and a stamp.

'Dearest Adam, look,' she wrote, 'the colour of the cloth is exactly the same as your dress. Where on earth did you find it! This one is beautiful too, but they've got it hanging on a wall, so no-one wears it any more. It's 250 years old, but it's still the loveliest thing. Ant says it's just a kimono, but what would he know?! With all my love, your sweetest little coffee girl in the morning, Amanda.'

Antony had written, 'Adam, she's telling fibs. It's not just a kimono, it's a kimono for a beautiful girl. She's sitting right here in front of me, right now. Thanks for helping me find her, Ant.'

It was just a blue silk dress, worn by a beautiful girl.

Gabriela - Twelve Silken Buttons

Closing Day

"I'll take the counter this morning, if you like," said Gabriela, pulling her black hair back in a twist and flicking a band around the thick coil. She inspected her red lips in the mirror, stretching out her fingers to see the same colour red on her nails. Gabriela hoped he liked red. She'd bought the matching colours the night before, and found herself thinking of the tall, silver haired man who came into the café most mornings.

"Yes, that would be good," replied her boss, Ruth. She looked across at Gabriela and smiled, amused at the younger woman preening in the mirror. She reached over and adjusted Gabriela's collar, spreading the lapels wider to reveal a delightful spray of freckles on her upper chest. Like a lotus branch in a beautifully etched Japanese print, the spray descended into the divide of Gabriela's divine cleavage. "Just one button," warned Ruth, "discreet, but enticing enough for their morning eye." She made one final correction to Gabriela's collar. "Perfect."

Being a savvy business woman, Ruth knew the importance of attractive staff behind her counters. Little Amanda had been wonderful, but she and her boyfriend were travelling overseas, so Ruth was grooming Gabriela to take her place. She was pleased with the young woman's slightly exotic appearance, a touch of Asia perhaps, or maybe South America. Some ancestral trace gave Gabriela dark, dark eyes and a darkness on her skin.

There was also a touch of something else about Gabriela, some ethereal essence Ruth couldn't quite put her finger on. Something about the young woman was, well, different. Ruth had a bit of the witch about her as all women do, and the sight some call intuition, some call second; but Gabriela... Ruth couldn't grasp it, and that made her curious.

Ruth had seen Adam's eyes narrow the first time he saw Gabriela, a sharper focus, just as they did when Amanda enticed him with her morning smile. Ruth wondered how long it would be before Gabriela tried her own witchery on Adam, for he was the kind of man who paid attention to his women, and they wanted that. Ruth could see from the way he talked to her girls, and the way he laughed with the woman with the long blonde hair, that he gave each of them his undivided attention. Each moment, theirs alone.

Even Ruth, who was older and wiser than all her girls, even Ruth couldn't resist his smile. She'd caught herself playing with her hair... Being the boss, Ruth could place a touch of possession on his arm when he was in her café, but wasn't so sure of herself outside her own space. Ruth enjoyed Adam's under-stated confidence and liked his presence in the café, as did her girls. Ruth suspected he gathered attention in most rooms he walked into, in his quiet way.

"Good morning, Adam. Is it your usual this morning?" Gabriela smiled up at him, the corners of her eyes genuine. "It's a latte, isn't it?"

"Yes it is, Gabriela, yes it is. One day I'll surprise us both and order something different." Adam looked upon the girl and saw her lips. He passed her the change, brushing her fingers with his, and saw the colour of her nails. "But not today."

"Look, the right money. You always bring the right money." Gabriela rang up the sale, glancing behind him. There was no line. "Will you be coming back later?"

"Later today, do you mean?" Adam replied. "No, probably not." He saw a flash in her eyes, something quicker than thought. "Why do you ask?"

"Oh, I just wanted to make sure I said goodbye before I go. Today's my last day before the holidays, I'm not in tomorrow." Gabriela looked straight at Adam and took in a breath. The shadow between her breasts tightened.

"Thank you," he said, "that's lovely, that you wanted to say goodbye to me. Are you going anywhere over the break?"

"Yes, I'm going home for Christmas, Christmas with the family." Gabriela touched the buttons on the cuff of her sleeve, and Adam saw her fingers turn.

Adam smiled as he fully registered her nails matched the red of her lips. "Will you be back in the New Year, then?"

"Yes. The café is shut for the next two weeks, after tomorrow, but I'll be here when we re-open."

"Well, I'll see you then." Adam heard the door behind him open. "Can you wait?"

She laughed. "I'll have to, won't I?"

"Yes, you will!" Adam moved aside for the next customer. "Have a lovely holiday, Gabriela. I'll see you soon."

On the flight between cities Gabriela sat in an aisle seat, just in front of the wing. As the cabin attendant did the safety drill Gabriela found herself admiring the woman's firm thighs and taut ass. The attendant stood right beside Gabriela, her crotch at eye level. Her slacks were tight fitting, and Gabriela admired the little curve of belly descending into the V at the top of her long legs. Gabriela was so close to the woman, she could have undone the belt and slid her hand around...

Gabriela closed her eyes, resting her hands on her own belly, a little curvier than the cabin girl's. She dozed lightly, semi lucid, and found herself re-playing the conversation with Adam that morning, saying goodbye to him. Goodbye also meant a hello later, and Gabriela imagined the soft look on his face when he saw her again. As she shifted her head from one side of the headrest to the other in a sleepy turn, Gabriela's fingers caressed her belly. In her dozing mind, she saw Adam's hands take up a cup and she saw the curve of the cabin girl's ass. Something mingled and was made in her mind. Desire.

Gabriela drifted in and out of sleep during the flight, and by the time the plane landed, she had a whole conversation ready for when she next saw Adam. She wondered if he liked her, until she realised of course he did. That's lovely, that you wanted to say goodbye to me. His words echoed and gave her peace of mind. Gabriela stretched out her fingers in front of her, admiring her red finger nails. She momentarily wished her fingers were a little longer, then turned her hands over and forgot about it.

Gabriela stood and reached for her bag in the overhead locker.

"Here, let me help." The young man in the seat opposite was already standing, lifting his own bag down.

"Thank you, that's very kind." Gabriela smiled at him.

"No problems. Come on Dad, let's go."

Every son has a father, thought Gabriela; every daughter, too. The older man looked across at her and his eyes creased, a quick glance down to her lips and back to her eyes.

Gabriela's return smile was an automatic response, the fractional tilt of her head a sub-conscious recognition of his appreciation. She took her bag from the boy, and looked again at the man.

That's lovely. Adam's voice was in her head. Gabriela smiled at the thought of him. The boy's father thought the smile was for him, but it wasn't. Not today.

"Hello Dad, thanks for picking me up. Mum not with you?"

"No darling, you know what she gets like before Christmas. The kitchen's out of bounds and I just do as I'm told. It's safer that way." Gabriela's father closed the car boot and turned to his daughter, his eyes soft at the sight of her. "How's my darling Gabs? It's been too long, honey, I've missed you."

Gabriela hugged her father close, her arms wrapped hard around his back, squeezing him tight. "Me too, Daddy, I know I should come back more often, but I'm always so busy." She tilted her head up and gave him a quick kiss on the lips, then buried her head in the crook of his shoulder; always her safest place, even when she was a little girl. "I'm home now, though. It's good to be back."

"You're by yourself again," her father said. "When..."

"Oh Daddy, don't. Not now. Mum is impossible, not you too."

Gabriela's father studied his daughter and didn't understand how this vibrant woman was always alone. As a girl at school she'd had the usual crushes, slammed doors and a repeated broken heart. He knew there were a number of disappointed boys, and later, sobbing girls writing bad poetry for her, and they were all good kids. Gabriela left a trail behind her, but kept walking. Had he brought her up to be too independent?

"It's OK, Daddy, don't fuss. I'm fine. I'm just not interested."

Gabriela's father knew his daughter well enough not to probe. He would take her side when her mother, as she inevitably would, took up arms against their daughter's single status. "Leave her be, Elizabeth, leave her be," he'd say. "She'll be fine, you'll see. She just hasn't met the right person yet."

Gabriela sometimes wondered about herself, but didn't fret. As a teenager she had put up with fumbles in the back seats of cars and movie theatres and later in bedrooms, given boys hand jobs and the occasional blow job, wiping cum from her hand. But whenever it came to her own pleasure, she found her partners to be too young, too inexperienced, and she kept putting away her virginity, saving it for another day, another man. She left her teens with it still intact and proceeded into her early twenties quite unfussed about its presence. She just hadn't met the right person yet.

She didn't dwell on it. She had prepared in her mind some words to calm her mother down, when the inevitable questions came. Gabriela's father, she knew, would be in her corner with his shoulder the perfect height for her to rest her head on, his arm around her back.

They chatted about this and that, and Gabriela remembered just how comfortable she was around her dad. She looked across at him, his concentration on the road ahead. Even though he was driving, she put her fingers to his cheek, grazing the stubble there. I love you, Dad, she thought. Her father looked across at his daughter beside him, his Gabs, and his heart melted as it always had, from when she was the tiniest thing, her eyes flashing with her stubbornness and passion for everything. He didn't need to say anything at all. Gabriela knew his love was always there for her, just her.

The next two days were chaos and Christmas; too much eaten on the day and eaten too late, presents placed under the tree and Gabriela's father playing Santa, ho ho ho, then Gabriela was exhausted. The end of the year caught up with her and she slept, long and dreamless, the heat flaying her naked body under the sheet.

When her father went in later to turn off her bedside light, he smiled when he saw Gabs' hand clutching her old faithful teddy.

"Elizabeth," he said to his wife, "it's just as well we kept all those old toys for the grandkids..."

"But we've got no grandchildren," she complained, "Gabriela won't..."

"Hush," he replied, "don't." He was gentle, but wasn't prepared to let her start. "I was going to say, just as well we kept them. Gabs is in there, remember her old favourite Ted? She's clutching its paw in her hand." He paused. "She's gorgeous. Our twenty-five year old daughter, and she's still got her little teddy." Gabriela's father stopped and pondered. "Sometimes, she's still my little girl, then she's all grown up." He shook his head. "My little Gabs, my darling Gabriela."

The next day Gabriela slept late, her parents moving around the house as quietly as they could. In the afternoon, Felicity, her oldest, closest friend from her school days came over. They had known each other since they were fifteen, and Flick was always welcome in the house. Back then she was a permanent fixture, and now Gabriela's parents made a fuss whenever they saw her.

"Hi, Mr and Mrs G. It's been a while. I only see you when Gabs comes back home, which she does less and less now."

"I know. It's a shame really, but what can we do? Gabriela insists on living interstate. We wonder what she's hiding, sometimes."

"Mum, god, I'm not hiding anything! How many times do I have to tell you?"

"Tell us what, darling?"

"There isn't anybody. Grrr, how many times, Mum!" Gabriela gave her usual response and her mother eventually let it go.

In Gabriela's Room

Later, up in Gabriela's room, Flick asked, "is there anyone Gabs, who you're interested in, even remotely?"

"Even remotely?" Gabriela paused. "Well yes, there is. Sort of."

Felicity didn't say a word, and continued to plait Gabriela's hair into a thick braid.

"Kind of," said Gabriela, articulating something in words for the first time. She'd thought it, but had never actually said anything out loud to anyone. But she could tell Flick anything, everything. "But nothing's happened. We chat, when he comes into the café, but that's all."

Felicity waited. Her fingers pulling and teasing on Gabriela's hair, she loved the soft feel of it, and it brought her close to her dearest friend. Her fingers caressed the hair, and every now and then she brushed it to her lips. Gabriela's eyes were closed as she luxuriated in the deep massage of her scalp, and never saw.

"Have you said anything to him," Flick asked, curious. She knew Gabriela's history with men, how she passed them by.

"Not really. Sort of," Gabriela replied. "I did make sure he knew I wanted to say goodbye to him, before the holidays."

"Really? What did he say?"

Gabriela remembered every word. "He asked, can I wait?"

"Wait for what, Gabs? What will you have to wait for?"

"Do you know," pondered Gabriela, "when it comes down to it, I don't know what I'll have to wait for..."

"It sounds to me, Gabs, you might have a crush on this man. Is he worth it, do you think?"

Gabriela was silent. Her pause was so long and unusual that Felicity stopped braiding her hair, and the stillness in the room somehow shifted and twisted with revelation.

"I think," said Gabriela slowly, "you're right. He might be absolutely worth it. Worth everything."

Felicity's fingers started their movement again and she thought of ceremonies and sacrifices. "You will tell me, won't you?" she asked, "when something happens."

"When something happens? But nothing's happened."

"You'll have to wait then, won't you?" said Flick, tying Gabriela's hair off with a band.

The young women loved each other's company, it was as if Gabriela had never gone away. They'd laughed and cried together for a decade; surviving, as so many girlfriends didn't, those years immediately after school when friendships ruptured and lives moved on. They often pondered it, "did you hear about... did you know that... I always knew she was..." and came to the conclusion it was their differences that kept them together.

There was something else too, that began as teenage girl curiosity and became a regular ritual, sustaining them both, drawing them closer each time. A necessary thing. "Promise, Felicity, we'll always do this, whatever happens. Even when we're sixty. Promise."

"Do women bleed, Gabriela? That's my promise."

It began simply, teenage girls comparing themselves, then young women discovering themselves, then adults enjoying themselves. "When we're sixty, it'll be a celebration."

It always began slowly.

Gabriela turned to Felicity and pulled her to her feet. Standing side by side in front of a floor length mirror, they compared their heights. At fifteen, Gabriela had been taller, but was slowly overtaken by Flick so now there were several inches difference in their heights. Flick was a slender woman, small breasted and long boned, athletic. Gabs was curvier, her waist small. She favoured long flowing skirts that swirled from her hips, her breasts shifting beautifully as she turned, brushing against Flick's arm.

"You do that every time," Flick commented. "You just have to do it, don't you?"

"Do what, darling? Oh, my lovely full breasts swaying in my bra, brushing up against your arm. Do I make you jealous, lovely girl, with your perky tits all tight and firm, but oh so small?" Gabriela's eyes sparkled, she loved this teasing play. "God, you're a bitch. Look at you, twenty five and you still don't need a bra."

Gabriela's eyes darkened and she licked her lips. "Come here, honey, come here." Her voiced deepened, husky with anticipation. "Let me see you."

She reached her hands to the waist of the taller woman and eased the tee shirt from Flick's tight jeans. Slowly Gabriela pulled the cloth up Flick's body, trembling slightly as she did so. Her movement was slow and teasing, they were in no hurry. She licked her lips again, and tilted her head up to Felicity's mouth. Their lips touched, and Gabriela's hands stopped. Their kiss was gentle at first, tentative. They remembered their first kiss, when there was a sweet innocence between them. But then the hungrier older women soon took over and their tongues thrust deeper.

Flick sucked Gabriela's lush bottom lip into her mouth, nipping it with her small teeth, tasting the linger of the red lipstick Gabriela wore. "Strawberry lips, I can taste the blood of strawberries on your lips."

Hearing her words, Gabriela wanted nipples like berries between her teeth. She quickly pulled Felicity's tee over her head, revealing those high, tight tits with big full nipples, succulent. "God, Flick, let me," and she pushed the other woman down onto the bed, her mouth following hungrily those perfect nubs, sucking first one into her mouth then the other. Gabriela opened her mouth wide around Felicity's breasts, sucking in as much of each tight, hard tit as she could.

Flick moaned and her body twitched with the sharp pleasure. Her hands were frantic too, reaching for the buttons on Gabriela's blouse, trying to undo them quickly. "Too many buttons, Gabs, too many." Her fingers fumbled, but she pulled and tugged, and the blouse opened wide, revealing Gabriela's lush, dropping breasts, barely contained in her bra. "Oh, god I love your breasts, your big swaying breasts."

She reached for the open front of the blouse, pushing it back from Gabriela's arms to reveal all of her friend's deep cleavage and the lovely roundness of the belly below. "Ohhh, Gabs, let me." Felicity pulled the curvaceous woman down to her body, feeling those soft mounds against her tight nipples, the soft belly against her harder, tighter gut, but always soft lips, so sweet. Flick fought with Gabriela's blouse, pulling it down her arms, desperate to get it off.

Gabriela pushed herself away from her girlfriend's body, sitting up high, gripping Felicity's hips between her thighs. She bent back away from Felicity's groping hands, teasing her arousal, laughing as she batted those hands away. "Darling Flick, what's the matter, can't you reach me, my glorious tits?" She held both breasts in her hands, offering herself up to the other woman, delighted in the effect she was having on Felicity. "Do you want to see me, all wonderful and naked?" Her voice was a sing song, and she whispered, "do you want my lush nipples between your lips?"

"Fuck, Gabriela, you know I do. Show me, bitch, show me."

"Oh Felicity, that's no way to speak to your oldest, dearest friend, not a polite way at all. Bitch?" Her eyes sparkled, revelling in the helpless woman trapped between her thighs. "I'm not a bitch. Just for that, I'm not going to show you!" Gabriela reached behind her back, quickly unclipping her bra, then brought her hands up under the cloth, hiding her breasts from Felicity's hungry eyes. She pressed hard against her own breasts, easing the ache developing behind her hard nipples.

"Gabriela, please, please let me see, please," Felicity pleaded, caressing the waist of the ripe body above her.

Gabriela leaned forward, taking her hands away from her breasts, and their weight swung them low over Felicity's head, just out of reach of her lips. She pulled the bra away from her arms and dropped it on the bed. Her full breasts swayed beneath her body. "Ahhh, Flick, here they are, all full and hot for you. My nipples, look, see how hard they are, just for you." She lowered herself some more, and Felicity suckled a tight nipple into her hot mouth, sucking and gently biting on the nub.

Gabriela moaned with delight and after some seconds, offered up her other breast for suck. "Oh yes, that's right, suck my breasts hard, oh, lovely girl. God, I love this, hmmmm."

For minutes they pressed their breasts against each other, taking turns to nip and suck and bite. Their first frantic undress slowed and they found themselves lying on their sides, their hands and fingers slow caresses. Gabriela held her beloved friend's face in her hands and gazed upon Felicity, soaking in her high cheeked beauty with her eyes. That was how their love started many years before, holding each other's young bodies, close and innocent, comparing themselves.

Felicity loved the heavy weight of Gabriela's breasts, and slid her fingers along her deep cleavage, twisting firm nipples between her finger and thumb, tracing the spray of freckles. Their movements slowed between them, leaving slow sensation and lingering touches.

"What are men's hands like, Flick? I don't know."

Gabriela wondered now, having left boys behind many years before and never finding a man who would take his time with her, a patient man. A longing was building up in her, a curiosity; some uncoiling thing to break down the small dread inside her, a vague fear time was passing by and leaving her behind.

Flick was the only woman she had known intimately, almost as well as she knew herself, but at least Gabriela knew the sexual pleasure a woman could bring. She couldn't remember the fumbling boys from her teens, but the idea of a man who knew how to seduce her, ah now, that was something different.

"A man's hands, Gabs?" Felicity pondered. "I don't know how to describe the difference, not really."

She looked at her own hands. "Bigger. Longer fingers. Sometimes gentle, sometimes not. I don't really know." Felicity thought back to their earlier conversation. "You might have to wait, Gabriela."

She was silent for a moment, then intuition hit her. "This man from the café, Gabs. Has he really noticed you, do you think?" Her own hands stopped moving on Gabriela's breasts. "What are his hands like?"

"Warm. Even on winter mornings, they're warm."

"I meant what they look like, long fingers or short, wide hands or what." Felicity laughed. "But you tell me you know they're warm already!"

Felicity moved her hands down Gabriela's belly to the waist of her skirt, sliding down the zip she found there, probing their way inside

Gabriela's knickers. "I think Gabs," she lowered her voice, "I think you might need to make this man see more of you. That's what I think."

Gabriela shivered with the run of Felicity's fingers over her clit, partly from Flick's light touch and partly from the idea of Adam. Adam. His fingers trailing over her belly, like Felicity's? Could she imagine it?

"What should I do? I don't know what to do, not with a man."

"Oh Gabriela," Flick replied, "I think you'll do just fine, if he saw you with your gorgeous curves and your red lips." She undid the button on Gabriela's waist band and tapped her on the bottom. "Lift your bum, so I can get this off."

As she slid the skirt down Gabriela's legs, Felicity sat up and looked at the woman lying abandoned before her. Gabriela's throat was flushed red with her arousal, and the top of her chest too, the blush darkening the freckles between her breasts. Her nipples were dark brown nubs, hard and tight, standing up from smooth skin. Between her sprawling legs, the crotch of her panties was a spread of dark wetness.

"Gabs, a man, finally. Are you ready for a man?" Felicity's voice was high and playful, teasing, but she knew this was a serious matter. Her darling Gabriela, wanting a man now? "Who is this man, Gabs? Describe him for me." Reaching down to Gabriela's waist, Flick peeled the wet knickers down. "Oh fuck, the lucky bastard," she whispered, "he's going to have that. So wet."

Gabriela's sex was dark between her legs, a fine tangle of black hair coiled tight along her lips, a slick of wetness shining. Her sex was lush and opening, a butterfly of inner lips rising from the darker outer pair. Felicity looked, long and hungrily, then slowly spread the inner lips to reveal a darker red, almost purple. "The lucky man," she repeated, "a paradise awaits." She slowly ran her fingers into Gabriela's cunt, finding her rough spot and pressing there. "Make sure he finds this place," she said, as Gabriela arched her back in ecstasy.

Felicity eased her fingers from Gabriela's hot sex, knowing she'd tease Gabriela and return there. But not yet. There was more she wanted to know about Gabriela's mystery man.

"Nooo, don't go, that's so good." Gabriela clenched her thighs together to trap Flick's hand, but the other woman was relentless and pulled away.

Flick needed to know more about this man. She wasn't exactly jealous, but it was something close. "What's his name, Gabriela? Tell me his name."

They'd had long conversations like this before, slowly circling around the topic of discussion, interrupting themselves with a kiss or playful tickle, giggling and gasping between their sheets, until finally they were beyond words and the only sounds in the room were low moans and sighs. But this was serious. Gabriela had never spoken about a man like this before, and Felicity needed to know more about him. She needed to approve.

"Adam. Come back to me, Flick. Don't go." Gabriela didn't want to trade pleasure for information, but sometimes there was no pleasing Flick. "His name's Adam."

Flick's fingers grazed across Gabriela's clit as a reward, sliding pleasure up into her throbbing cunt, connecting the image of this man in Gabriela's mind with desire and lust, cunt proud and deep.

Felicity sensed a change in her friend. She wanted Gabriela to want a man, to be filled and full. She grazed her fingers down the long slide of Gabriela's wetness. "How old is he, Gabs?"

"How old? Oh, fuck, your fingers, they feel so good." Gabriela keened with pleasure and struggled for words. "He's... He's... Jesus Flick, you're wicked, stop... he's... I don't know, fifty." Her breath caught up, "older maybe, ohh."

"Fifty, Gabs?" Felicity's fingers continued their pressure, sliding the start of a slow fuck into Gabriela's clenching cunt, pushing the idea of cock into her. "He's old enough to be your father."

"I know. Is it wrong?" Gabriela bucked her hips up, clenching Flick's fingers inside her.

"Oh no, Gabs, every girl loves her Daddy, don't you think?" Felicity fucked two fingers deep into Gabriela's sliding cunt.

"He's not my father, Flick, he's... Adam, he's... Oh Flick, fuck, stop, you're teasing me." She moaned, and cried out his name. "Adam, he's..."

Felicity was satisfied. "Sshhhh, my darling, no more questions." She leaned down to Gabriela's mouth, her kiss and darting tongue a reward, and her fingers sliding around Gabriela's clitoris a promise. "Ssshh, lovely girl. Let me. I want to."

Felicity gazed down at Gabriela, her legs spread wide on the bed, her throat and chest flushed; and she loved her sweet friend so much, so very much. She ached inside, and nearly wept, but Gabriela's pleasure was all that mattered now. Felicity cared nothing for herself at this moment, Gabriela was her purpose and her prize.

And Adam's prize. Felicity didn't know this man, but trusted Gabriela in her choice of him. But who would seduce who? How would Adam know?

Gabriela looked up at Flick and saw something in the other woman's eyes, flickers of emotion running through her. She reached up her arms in a wide embrace. "Come to me, Flick. I'll tell you, I promise, but it's us now, just us. I love you, Flick, don't ever forget it. You're my first girl."

"But you've found a man, Gabs."

"Don't be jealous, Flick, he couldn't ever be like you." As was always the way with their deepest, most intimate conversations, conclusions were reached and promises made. Gabriela realised what her words meant. Adam was inevitable, and he didn't even know. Witches were at work, spells being woven like a tapestry, a cloak; spells sewn like the finest embroidery, a web, a veil.

"No, I'm not jealous. Envious maybe." Felicity paused. "Gabriela, did you know, back then, what saying no to all those boys meant?"

"No, I don't think so. They just weren't right for me, that's all I knew."

"Adam's right though, isn't he?" Flick thought of practicalities. "How will he know?"

"Tomorrow, Flick, we'll go buy me a dress. If I'm going to try to catch his attention I'll need a dress, a beautiful dress." She pictured herself. "A long flowing dress, tight at the waist."

With that thought in her head, Gabriela reached for the waist of Flick's tight jeans and undid the single button there. "Lift your bum," she said, "so I can peel these things off you. Too much talk, Flick. We always talk too much, don't we?"

They stopped talking, but the room wasn't silent for long.

Later, in the still of the night. Gabriela's father made his round of the house, like he always had since Gabs was tiny, checking the outside doors were locked and all the lights were off. He saw light under the door to Gabriela's room, and knocked gently. Hearing silence, he softly opened the door and went to the bedside table to turn the lamp off.

"Pull the covers up Daddy, I'm cold." Gabriela's sleepy voice was just a tiny whisper, her words automatic, triggered by his presence.

He looked down at the two women lying naked, back to back on the bed. He smiled as he gently covered them with the sheet, not wanting to wake them.

"G'night, Gabs," he whispered, "love you."

"Love you back, Daddy." Their night time words, always, but she was asleep, Flick too.

He left the room, quietly shutting the door behind him. He wouldn't say anything to Elizabeth, but wouldn't forget the sight of them, either.

The First Day Back

"Gabriela, hello. It's good to see you. Did you have a good break?"

Adam greeted the young woman warmly, remembering she had gone back to her family for Christmas.

"Yes, it was lovely to see Mum and Dad. I slept most of it, though."

"Lucky girl. But now back into it, yes?"

"Yes. A new year. New promises, new things." She smiled up at him. "But you, back here again? It's a latte still?"

"Yes, it's still a latte." He gave her the right money, and her fingers were warm. "I'm quite predictable, I'm afraid."

"But I always remember your order though, that's useful."

"I guess it is, useful."

As he turned from the counter, he noticed Gabriela touch the buttons on her cuff, and thought it a familiar gesture, but couldn't quite place it. Then he remembered. Before the holidays, when she said goodbye to him, she had made the same gesture. It seemed almost a nervous thing.

As he waited for the barista to brew the coffee, he admired Gabriela from behind. She was efficient, her hands busy with the till and change, but she was hidden behind another counter, so he could see only her profile, the fall of her hair, her back. And the ridge of the bra across her back. Idly, he wondered if her bra was red, to match her lips. He smiled to himself. How would he ever find out?

The barista called Adam's name, and he took the coffee. As he turned outside the door, he glanced back. Gabriela watched him leave, her fingers twisting the buttons at her cuffs. Adam saw the movement and wondered if it was a subconscious thing. Her smile was for him, and he took it with him down the street.

Gabriela followed him with her eyes, and as she did so she reached inside her collar and adjusted the strap of her bra. She was aware of the weight of her breasts and the ache behind her nipples, and the shift of her flesh felt good. It was a conscious thing, because of him. Her bra was a pale shade of blue, a nice contrast to her dark skin.

That night, Gabriela rang Flick. "I don't know what to do. I've seen Adam, but how do I get him to see me outside the café? How do I say something?"

"You need to get him somewhere where he can see you in the dress. Once he sees you in the dress, he'll be interested." Felicity paused, and the line hissed with distance. "What time do you get off work? Could you get away an hour or so earlier on a Friday? Meet him somewhere?"

"I guess. I can ask Ruth. Tell her I've got a doctor's appointment or something."

"That would work. Meet him a couple of blocks away from your work. Somehow suggest drinks."

Gabriela could tell from Felicity's staccato speech she was thinking as she was talking.

"A drink. What's a good celebration?" The logic of Felicity's thinking caught up with her. "A doctor's appointment won't work." The line went quiet. "You just need to be a damsel in distress. That always works in books."

"It's not a book, Flick. That won't work." Gabriela was disheartened. "Grrr. How can I make him see me, outside work?"

"What time does he finish? Bump into him as he walks past."

"What? No, surely that won't work. It's too obvious."

"It works in books, Gabriela, so you can make it work."

"The way you're talking, I need a library." There was a long silence. "Are you there, Flick?"

"Yes. Too much thinking, Gabs, we're thinking too much."

"What do you mean?"

"Simple is best. Just give him your phone number, Gabs. On a piece of paper. Easy." Felicity laughed. "Who's not going to call you? If a woman gives a man her phone number, of course he's going to call."

Adam unfolded the piece of paper, smoothing it out in his palm. Her name, Gabriela, was written in a looped, feminine hand, together with her number.

"Adam," she'd said, her voice low and her eyes looking down. "Please, I'd like you to call me. I've..."

He remembered her earlier words and the nervous movement of her fingers around the cuffs of her blouse. He'd taken the tightly folded paper quickly between his fingers, and touched it to his lips. The movement pulled her eyes to his face, and he mouthed the words, I will, saving her from her own fear and fuelling his own curiosity.

He wondered at her action, and felt she was brave doing it, or terrified. Perhaps both. He didn't know what she wanted, but thought she must want it keenly. The next steps, wherever they might lead, were now his to make it easier for her.

"Gabriela, hello. It's Adam. You wanted me to call. Is it a good time?"

"Yes. Adam. It's me. I..." She didn't know what to say next. "Can I..."

"Gabriela, how about I pick you up somewhere, and take you somewhere else? You can ask me then, when you're not rushed." Adam took control. "When can you be ready? And where?"

There was a silence on the line for a moment, then Adam heard an intake of breath, and she gave him her address, and a time. "Is that time OK? Does it suit you?" Now that Gabriela had made up her mind, clocks were ticking and time was everywhere.

Adam was slower, more patient. In his world, time always slowed and spiralled inwards towards a moment. He was intrigued, no doubt: what did the young woman want? Did she come bearing gifts or seeking offerings? He instinctively thought of a still place, a quiet place, where she could slow herself down. The image of fingers twisting and turning on the cuffs of her blouse caught in his head and he wondered about that.

In the Garden

He walked to the step of her door, a small townhouse on the south side, with a tiny walled garden. Frangipani brushed his sleeve and he was scented by her flowers. Adam was aware of a heat low in his groin and his senses tightened. His vision sharpened, and he breathed in deeply the sweet scent of the flowers. He heard movement on the other side of the door, and stepped back.

Gabriela opened the door and Adam saw her silhouette framed there, the small curve of her waist the perfect width for his hands if they danced, but they weren't dancing yet. He reached out his hand to escort her over her own threshold, and she rested her fingers on his. Adam raised her hand to his lips, and it was the perfect gesture.

"Nobody's ever done that before," she said, "it's my first time for that."

"Gabriela," he replied, "it won't be the last."

He turned and she followed, pulling the door shut with a solid clunk. Her past closed behind her.

"Come, I know a lovely place." Adam gave her his arm, and escorted her to the car, her dress flowing with movement. "Your dress, it's beautiful." Gabriela's eyes shone, she must tell Flick everything he said.

"Thank you," she said, "this is the first time I've worn it."

"It's a special occasion then." Adam looked down at her, "And I'm the lucky man to be seen with you." He opened the passenger door, admiring her legs as she swung them into the car. He reached for the seat belt, for the pillar was a long way back, and passed it to her. He watched as Gabriela took the buckle in her hand and clicked it in place, and he saw two buttons on the cuff. Her wrist was delicate. Her hair was coiled high on her head in a twist, escaping strands soft and dark against her throat.

Adam took in a breath and began to see all of her, assembling a collection of glances into a complete vision of a woman. He moved around the front of the car, so she could see him.

"Have you been to the Japanese Garden, Gabriela, on the edge of the parklands?"

"No, but I've heard about it."

"It's a quiet place. It'll suit you." Adam started the car. "It's exotic and slightly mysterious." He glanced across at her and wanted to reach out and touch her cheek, to prove she was real. But he didn't, afraid she might vanish, not real.

"Am I?" she echoed, "exotic and slightly mysterious?" She looked across at him, and wanted to touch his cheek, but he wasn't her father so she couldn't. "I've never been called that before."

"Another first then. So many firsts, Gabriela." He slowed, and turned onto a road running beside the parkland, trees in the distance and hills beyond. "I'm beginning to think I'm your first man." He glanced at her, and saw the sudden twist of her hands in her lap.

Gabriela, startled by his words, took in a deep breath and felt a sharp stab deep within her breasts. Her nipples felt huge, as if every nerve pulsed there, and she knew if she pressed her hand to her flesh, her nipples would be hard, hot hard. She felt heat in the base of her belly, and her sex bloomed and opened. Her senses felt visceral and raw, and she saw veins threaded on the back of Adam's hand. A tiny pulse beat there, beating blue.

And so they awoke to each other's presence. Gabriela knew instantly her choice was right; and Adam sensed he was chosen, but he knew not for what.

Adam brought the car to a stop, and they turned to each other.

"Hello, Gabriela, finally. You're here now."

"Yes, Adam. I am. I'm here, with you. I like it."

"Come then, my lovely, let's go to the garden and we can walk. Then we can sit and talk." He gazed into her eyes. "You can tell me what it is I can do for you."

He knows, Gabriela thought, he knows I want him, but he can't know for what.

She's chosen me for something, wondered Adam, but what?

The Garden was a gift from a sister city, and was a small, self contained enclosure separated from the bare grass paddocks by hedges and high fences. Water surrounded an island that could be reached by flat stone bridges. Circuitous paths meandered through exquisite vistas, cleverly designed and contemplative, each turn perfectly constructed for the view beyond. It was well established, with tall pines casting shade and keeping the walks cool.

Other than Adam and Gabriela, it was deserted. A gentle breeze blew warm against their skin, and Gabriela's dress swirled and lifted as she walked. They went side by side silently for a while. Adam, who knew the garden, set a slow pace; and every now and then Gabriela would stop as they turned a corner and saw a new miniature landscape, a rock for a mountain, a tree for a forest.

"It's so clever how it's laid out. Each stopping place has a perfect view." She looked up at Adam, and leaned into his arm; the pressure not quite the weight of her head against his shoulder, but almost. "It's quiet, isn't it? The sound of the little waterfalls, it's just gorgeous."

She stepped away to look at him, this tall man in a quiet place, and wondered how he saw her.

The flow of her dress as Gabriela stood before him was like a veil of water falling. It was pale and cream, a contrast to her darker skin. The skirt of it flared over her hips and clinched into a tight waist, and the bodice hugged her full breasts pushed high. Adam counted eight buttons down the front, from high on her chest to just below the base of her belly, and two buttons on each cuff. Adam remembered her words, it's the first time I've worn it. The dress, then, was chosen especially for him.

Twelve silken buttons, and each to undo.

"Your dress, Gabriela, is beautiful. You're beautiful." Adam loved the brightness in her eyes and her smile as she heard his words. "Let's sit, that bench is shaded and cool."

The bench was under a timbered pergola, offering visitors a view of a raked gravel sea with islands of rock placed in a precise pattern, lichens and moss a tiny microcosm. Adam and Gabriela sat beside the sea. Tiny birds, wrens, substituted for seagulls and were tame, flitting to their feet then gone when no seed was dropped. Gabriela laughed at their quick, darting flight.

"Look, there's the male, bright blue." She touched Adam's arm, pointing. "See, on the branch."

Adam saw, but the young woman beside him interested him more. He said nothing, not knowing what she wanted. He knew this peaceful place would calm Gabriela, and when she was ready, she would find her words.

Gabriela wandered at first, telling him a little of home, a little of her work. Adam learned about Felicity, "My closest friend, she knows me so well," and saw the love in Gabriela's eyes for her.

"Will I meet her, your friend?"

"Oh maybe, one day. She knows about you..." Gabriela stopped, realising she had said too much. "I mean... I've mentioned you. One of my customers..." She stopped again, and looked at Adam for help. "Sorry, I'm..."

"Chattering?" Adam's voice was soft, gentle. He looked at the young woman beside him in her perfect dress, her hands gripped together in her lap to stop their movement. A sudden flash of instinct made him turn towards her, a quarter turn, and with one arm around her shoulder and a hand on her hair, he gently tilted her head so it rested in the crook of his shoulder, safe. "It's OK, lovely. Rest your head here. I've got you."

Gabriela sighed, tension spilling from her, and she relaxed against him. Slowly, she turned her head up towards his, her lips opening to just show her teeth. Adam looked down and saw her open mouth, her closed eyes, a faint flush on the side of her long throat. His lips touched hers, soft at first, then their tongues touched.

Gabriela's hand went to the back of Adam's head, pulling them together, and their kiss was long and sweet. Hungry but slow, their tastes mingled. Adam grew hard, and Gabriela was wet for him, but she wanted it to take forever, slowly and forever.

But first, Adam had to know. Gabriela pulled back and looked up at this man, this man who surely would know what to do. "Adam," she swallowed, and found some words. "Adam, this will sound strange, but..." Her hand touched the back of his hand on her shoulder for comfort. "I want... I need to tell you something. About me. You need to know something about me."

"What is it Gabriela, what do I need to know about you?" He caressed her hair slowly, calming her like a cat, waiting for her revelation. "It can't be bad, I wouldn't believe that." He kissed her again, to encourage her thoughts. "I'm sure I can cope." Adam smiled, but his blue eyes narrowed just a little, tell me.

Gabriela took in a deep breath, pressing her palm against his hand on her shoulder for strength. Adam stopped stroking her hair, and she knew she had to go on, to bring the comfort back, to get it done.

"This dress, Adam, It was Flick's idea. I..." She stopped. "No, I'm being silly. It doesn't matter."

"Doesn't matter, Gabriela? Are you sure?"

"Yes, I'm sure. It doesn't matter."

Gabriela changed the subject. "It's nice being here with you though, I'm glad you bought me here. It's peaceful."

Adam looked at her, having watched a myriad of emotions pass across her face. She said it didn't matter, whatever it was, but he could see that it was important. No matter, he was a patient man, he could wait. He would find out sooner or later, it was just a matter of time. Adam had plenty of that, and was used to a slow pursuit. It made a seduction more satisfying, the longer it took.

Adam gazed upon her still beauty, sitting there in her beautiful dress, and decided yes, he would put his mind to this woman. She was different to other women he had known, some essence in her wasn't the same. He was intrigued by her, and that made her interesting.

"May I, Gabriela?" Adam took one of her hands in his, and undid one button. His lips whisper kissed her wrist, and a tiny pulse heated the scent she had dabbed there earlier. Her scent rose, and Adam breathed it in deep. Her wrist was everything, it was the first moment of Gabriela's seduction, the first place.

In a Japanese garden, a thread of moments began, silken threads twisting around tightly; twelve silk buttons to be undone...

"Good god, Flick, his gentleness with me, I couldn't believe a kiss on the inside of my wrist could be so exquisite. Adam kissed my wrist, his lips like a butterfly quivering. That's all he did, Flick, there in the garden. I felt like those pictures of a hundred years ago, where the women flirt behind a fan and drop a handkerchief. He was so gentle, so delicate."

"What did he do next Gabs? What did he do?" Felicity wanted to know everything, every word, every tiny gesture. She couldn't wait.

"Goodness, Flick, you're so impatient!" Gabriela paused, teasing her darling girl, knowing what happened next and re-living it as she retold the moment. "Adam's so wicked, Flick. He knew exactly what to do."

"What, Gabs, what?"

"He undid another button, Flick, two buttons now. Both cuffs."

"Gabriela, you tart, you're shameless. Two!" Felicity could imagine the gorgeous smile on Gabriela's face, she could hear the joy in her friend's voice. "Oh, Gabs, can I have him when you're finished? I've never been undressed slowly, never. I'm so jealous." Felicity was worldly and knew men, but she'd never known a man like this man. "Oh Gabs, where did you find him?"

"In Ruth's café. In the mornings, just like that. Amanda served him first, and I could see how, when he spoke to her, nobody else existed. Then I served him for a week in a row. And he was the same with me. He'd talk to me, and all I wanted was for him to look at me again and again. It was only ever a minute or two, but I'd melt each time. I felt like a silly swooning school girl, but all I wanted was his smile. Just for me."

"And you wore red lipstick and matching nails. Gabriela, you're a total slut. You've started your witchy ways on him." Felicity was impressed. "How could he resist you?"

I couldn't resist you either, thought Felicity. Fuck, I'm jealous, she thought twice.

"When are you seeing him next, Gabs?"

I'm going to torture myself if he seduces her slowly, Felicity thought, thrice. And another witching woman awoke, and tendrils moved through the ether towards Adam, weaving a spell slowly.

Adam shivered, a ghost walking over his grave. He looked up, but no-one was there. It was a familiar touch, from long ago and tomorrow. He shook his head, clearing his thoughts.

His mind turned to Gabriela, and Adam pondered his next step. A long, slow approach might be best, tantalising and teasing, moving ever closer to the prize that was Gabriela, so many delightful stops along the way. He thought of those brilliant Japanese woodcuts from the nineteenth century, where seduction was hinted at behind closed screens, shadows and rain and blossoms falling.

Then Adam thought of another type of Japanese woodcut, where the sex was huge and joyous, with massive cocks and big hairy cunts, a maid stealing a glance from behind a screen, and luxurious cloth. Ah, so much inspiration.

And Gabriela herself, there was something divine and beatific about the young woman that entranced Adam, which made him adore her. He wanted so much to be held in her arms like some fallen angel, his own darkness purged by her grace, held safe. She wasn't the same as other women he had known, there seemed a different gentleness about her, some inner peace. He craved for it, to be held by her.

A Black Velvet Choker

"Gabriela, come, stand before me."

Adam gazed upon her as she stood before him, her hair long and dark and falling down over her breast, nearly to her waist. Her dress, as before, had swayed and swirled as she walked beside him, her heels clicking on the pavement. Now the flow of cloth was still, but the bodice swelled high with her breath.

From a pocket of his coat, Adam produced a black velvet box, and turned it towards her. Gabriela undid the small clasp, and lifted the lid.

"It's beautiful. Thank you."

"It's the first thing I'll place against your skin, Gabriela, and the last thing I shall take off. With it on, you'll stand nude before me; with it off, you'll stand naked." Adam moved towards her, lifting her face to his in a kiss. "If you'll let me, that is."

She stood still before him; and his fingers moved to the highest silken button on her bodice, undoing the button and revealing her throat. He swept the long weight of her hair into his hand, and coiled it up high and away from her neck. "Hold it up," he said, "and look at me."

Gabriela held her head tilted proud, and bared her throat to receive his gift. Adam took the black velvet choker from the box and undid its catch. He placed it around her throat and it was a narrow band of darkness against her dusky skin. He claimed her with it, and his promise of dropping it away from her skin was a sign of his confidence Gabriela didn't debate.

"Come, Gabriela, sit with me."

Gabriela sat beside him, and the buttons on her sleeves were undone, her wrists bare and slender. Adam took one hand in his, kissing the tips of her fingers one by one, then eased them, two at a time, into his mouth. His mouth was hot and her fingers heated. A nerve ran from each of her nipples to the base of her clit, and all three nerve centres peaked and tightened. Gabriela sighed, and fell against his chest, a hand against Adam's heart.

They kissed for a long moment, their tongues exploring each others' mouths. Gabriela crept sideways onto Adam's lap, half on and half off, and she felt his shaft hard against her thigh. She pressed herself against it, and was rewarded with a small intake of his breath. She pressed again, and took a tight tip of Adam's tongue into her mouth.

Gabriela closed her lips against the thrust of his tongue, and for the first time Adam forced her. She softened against his will and was not taken. She gave herself up, wanting him, her first time resisting him then letting the man in. Adam savoured the moment, and held her body against his.

Still curled on his lap, Gabriela touched the cuffs of Adam's shirt and undid the buttons, each cuff at a time. She said nothing, no permission sought, no permission given. Adam stretched out his arms to make it easier for her fingers, and she rolled each cuff up one turn. Gabriela took his fingers to her mouth and repeated the same tip suck that he gave her, and felt the length of his cock shift. She looked up at him, her eyes bright but less of a smile, concentrating on learning the length and angles of his fingers.

She splayed her hand against his broad palm, and her hand was smaller. She'd thought she wanted longer fingers, but his curled over the top of hers and interlaced, so it didn't matter. Their palms touched and were warm, and Adam placed his other hand over the back of hers and her hand was safe between his. Gabriela's free hand reached up to Adam's cheek and cradled his face. She watched his eyes close and felt an ever so slight change in the weight on her palm; and Gabriela knew some small tension in him was given up to her, that he too could soften and relax and sleep in her hands.

They were wordless, tiny flickerings of trust moving back and forth as their fingers made trails over skin and cloth and each other. Gabriela's eyes never closed, she took him all in, learning every small scar and line on his skin, learning a man.

Adam knew more, and was looking for something else, so his touch was different, less tentative. He undid two more of the silken buttons on the front of Gabriela's dress, and his fingers moved upon the upper curves of her full breasts, finding the divide of her cleavage and the long line to her throat. She was still curled on his lap so his exploration was uneven. Gabriela wriggled, wanting all of her skin to be touched, she was becoming hungrier now.

Adam gently turned, and lowered Gabriela to the couch so she lay there, her throat flushed, her mouth slightly open, oh for her sighs. He took a step back and stood upright and she lay before him, the long flow of the dress covering her legs, hiding her hips. Adam stood quite still for a moment, studying Gabriela, savouring her beauty, her quiet presence.

Gabriela's gaze on him was steady, she didn't look away, her eyes were black. Her eyes narrowed, so subtle he nearly missed it. A slight prickle went up the back of his neck, and what he thought was the want of her became a need for her. The air in the room shifted, and Adam felt a slight spin of vertigo. He tensed his legs, pushing down to the floor to steady himself, to catch his balance. Could she save him?

"Tell me, tell me, Gabriela, what happened next?" Felicity held the phone close to her ear, Gabriela's voice fading and falling with the distance, a faint echo doubling their voices, voices.

"He just looked at me, Flick, and it was like some strange light switched in his eyes. God, the way he looked at me." Gabriela's voice dropped to a whisper, as she remembered the moment. "The intensity of his gaze, I didn't know what it meant." She paused. "I just reached for him, I reached up to take him in my arms." Talking about it brought an explanation she'd not seen before.

"He seemed lost, Flick, so lost. I just wanted to hold him in my arms. So I did, Flick, I opened my arms to him and he came to me, and lay his head on my breast. Before, he'd held my hand in his, but now it was my turn to hold his hand between mine. His head on my breast, like a baby."

"What happened next, Gabs?" Flick whispered into her phone, not really believing what Gabriela was saying, but aching to hear every moment of it. She did not know Adam, but was astonished to hear of this intensity in the man, this vulnerability, and Gabriela's natural reaction.

"Did you just hold him forever, Gabs? This man of yours?" Felicity ached for a man like him, who needed a woman so much. She'd never found one.

"Not forever, but a long time. I think he almost slept on my chest. Then he stirred." Gabriela stopped talking, and Felicity could imagine the look on her face as she remembered. "Oh God, Flick, his care for me, I couldn't believe how gentle he was with me."

Adam hadn't slept. He'd listened to the quieting hush of Gabriela's heartbeat as it calmed to a steady beat. Her breath was even and slow, and she matched the slow caress of his hair, her hand over the curve of his skull, to her breathing. He felt a natural stillness in the woman, so at peace with herself that she calmed him, soothed him.

Gabriela was a resting place for Adam. There were times in his life when he met a woman unexpectedly, when he wasn't expecting anything or seeking anyone; when a woman simply arrived in his life. He might be drinking coffee, reading a paper, and would look up at a sound, a movement, even a shadow; and there she would be, a newcomer in his life. Inevitably, he would be seduced by the magic the woman wrapped around him until he was helpless like Merlin trapped in Nimue's tree, until she grew bored and set him free.

This time though, Gabriela sold him the coffee and cleared away the paper after he had gone, and he was the newcomer coming into her territory, her café. Perhaps it was a reversal of the roles this time, where he cast the shadow, where it was his movement through the door that made her look up, that turned the moment around. Was he simply arriving in her life? He'd not thought of it like that before. Was he Merlin unbound, this time?

There was a mystery to Gabriela he couldn't place, a hesitation in her and something tentative. Several times now Adam had seen her fingers twisting around her wrists in a nervous motion, repeated and repeated. But she knew when it was right to beckon him into her arms and simply hold him, and he wanted to be held by her.

Adam lay with his head on her chest, his cheek pillowed inside her shoulder. He could see the faint beat of a pulse on her throat and if he listened closely, her heartbeat by his ear. Adam pushed a curl of hair away from her neck and felt an intake of breath. He stroked his fingers gently against her throat and heard a faint sigh, and the tiny pulse on her skin quickened. Ah yes, Adam thought, her heart beats a little faster for me.

Gabriela's fingers gripped part of her dress, and her eyes fluttered closed. Her hand stopped moving through Adam's hair, and there was a second reversal in the room. Adam pushed himself up onto his elbows and looked down at the woman below him. Gabriela's eyes were closed, long lashes black, the colour in her skin rising. Her red lipped mouth was slightly open, her lips full and inviting. Adam kissed her softly, and her hand left the folds of her dress to find his, but his hand was gone.

Adam reached for a button on Gabriela's dress, two buttons undone down the front and now a third. The tops of her breasts were showing, the delightful spray of freckles descending into the shadow of her cleavage. The cut of the dress was deceptive, hiding the fullness of her breasts. With the buttons undoing, undone, her curves were full and enticing.

He passed a single finger down into the cleft, following the freckles but losing count, and was rewarded by a shiver of goose-bumps and another sigh, louder this time. Gabriela licked her lips, just the tip of her tongue, and Adam rewarded her with another kiss.

"Gabriela, we should eat. If I undo another button, we'll never make the restaurant on time." Adam got to his feet, and reached for her hands to pull her up. She swayed, and gripped his arm. "It's OK, I've got you."

He held her close for a moment, pulling her body to his and enjoying the press of his cock against her. He stepped back, placing both hands on her waist which was small. Gabriela delighted him, and Adam's eyes were blue, a smile in his eyes for her. She was real before him, not a dream. Adam adjusted the spread of her collar, pushing back the cloth to show her perfect cleavage. Gabriela smiled to herself and Adam saw it.

"Tell me. Am I amusing you?"

"No," replied Gabriela, "not at all. I was just thinking of Ruth's instructions."

"Ruth's instructions?"

"Yes. Just one button, she'd say. To entice them in the morning."

Gabriela saw herself in the mirror, and put her hand to her chest, spreading her fingers over the length of the buttons undone. "Three buttons, Adam. What would she think?"

"Clever woman, Ruth," Adam replied. "One for the morning, two by lunchtime, three buttons for dinner." He kissed her lips again, and wanted her.

Gabriela listened to the logic of his words, and knew there were five more buttons on this dress. Her breasts ached and her nipples were hard, and there were only three silken buttons undone on the bodice.

In the base of her belly Gabriela's wetness was full and ready, but he still didn't know she didn't know men. He was undoing her buttons one by one. She knew it was a seduction now, and she didn't know what to do.

"What did you do, Gabs?"

"I was tormented, is what I was, teased. I loved it."

Felicity lay back on her bed in her sweats. She'd just come in from a run when her phone rang and it was Gabriela, so she went straight to her room, dragging her runners and socks from her feet as she did so.

"He lay on my shoulder for I don't know, ten minutes, fifteen, I can't really say. Then it was just like another switch went click in his head. He didn't say a word, just started stroking my throat. God, Flick..."

Felicity lay there, picturing Gabriela with this man, wishing it was herself in their room. She was hot from her run, and peeled her top from her torso to reveal a simple tight sports bra, lines of sweat curved under her shallow breasts. Flick brushed her fingers through her short hair, pushing it away from her face.

"... my skin shivered with goose bumps when Adam ran his finger down my cleavage..."

"Wait, Gabs, how many buttons? Cleavage? How much cleavage?"

Flick was beyond curious, she wanted to know everything. It wasn't fair, here she was, fairly experienced with boys and men; and her sessions were clothes off, jump into bed, quick fuck, usually OK and sometimes she came. And there was Gabs who didn't have a clue, being romanced and charmed, seduced properly by someone who...fuck, someone she wanted. Someone who knew what he was doing. Felicity gripped the phone closer with one hand.

"Three buttons. I even measured the length of them with my fingers spread. But he's not even seen my bra yet, Flick. He's so polite, reaching down to pull me up from the couch, holding me steady." Gabriela paused, remembering. "Not so polite, really." She giggled.

"What Gabs? Why not polite, really?"

"Because when he held me close, I could feel him against my thigh." Gabriela paused, waiting for Flick's response.

"Against your thigh? That's a pretty close hug, Gabs."

"Not just a close hug, Flick, that's not what I meant."

"What are you ta...?" Felicity finally got it. "Jesus, Gabs, what the fuck, he's hard for you?"

"Don't sound so surprised, Flick. I can be pretty hot too, you know."

Gabriela flicked her hair back, and even though Flick was a thousand miles away, she knew exactly what look was on Gabs' face.

"Sorry baby, I know you can." Felicity was quick to calm her friend before she took off like a colt. Fuck, I'm so jealous, she thought.

Flick looked down at herself, and her nipples were hard and long, pushing up points through her bra. Her breasts ached, and between her legs her sex wettened and she knew what was going to happen next.

"Tell me, Gabs, what happened next?" Her voice was low, with a huskiness from her growing arousal.

Felicity peeled the bra over her head, and looked down to her long nipples, like the tips of her little finger, hard and tight. She cupped one palm over a breast and pushed hard to stop the ache. Her sex bloomed and she sighed.

"Was that you, Flick?" Gabriela's voice softened. She knew it was.

"Adam got my long grey coat from behind the door, and draped it over my shoulders. 'To keep you warm, Gabriela,' he said. He always calls me Gabriela. It's so sophisticated when he says it. Gabriela."

She paused, letting her friend picture them both together. "Then he escorted me to his car. Properly escorted me, Flick, opened the car door and everything, handed me the seat belt even."

Felicity twisted a nipple between a finger and a thumb, and pulled it tight, pinching a small pain into her breast. Oh h, that felt good. More. "Where did you go, Gabs? Tell me." Torment me, because it's not me, going in the car. "Wait."

Gabriela heard movement, and the single squeak of a bed spring, and she knew Flick was shifting on the bed, lifting her bum, no doubt, to pull her bottoms and knickers down. Gabs and Flick, they knew each other so well.

Gabriela pictured Flick's strong, toned belly, and the hard curve of muscle at the base of her gut, diving into plain cotton-tails, her sexy knicks, as Felicity called them. Down now, kicked off from the ankle, her long legs spreading wide, one knee bent, cooling her cunt to the air. Her long smooth sex was neater than Gabriela's little crinkled butterfly wings, her lips smooth and fine, a high clit exposed.

"We just went to a restaurant, Flick. A beautiful one, perfect food, we shared a bottle of wine. Adam knew the chef, who came out and made a fuss."

"What did he do, Gabs?" Felicity moaned, as she spread her lips and slid her fingers inside. "Tell me."

"We chatted, this and that. He listened to me." Gabriela was thoughtful. "He probably indulged me, let me go on about myself too much. And you, Flick, I told him some more about you."

Flick's fingers stopped sliding between her sex lips. "What did you tell him about me, Gabs?" Her fingers penetrated, and she started a slow fuck into herself, wet and slow. The idea of this man, even filtered and made fanciful through Gabriela's narrative, was penetrating deep into her mind, and she wanted him. Her fingers pushed.

"I told him we'd known each other since we were teenagers at school."

Felicity lay the phone on her pillow, and rolled onto her front. She raise her ass high, placing her weight on her knees, long, lean thighs spread apart. "What else, what else did you tell him about me?"

"I described you to him."

Felicity's fingers spread aside her lips and she wet her fingers, sliding them around and over the nub of her clit. Pleasure started to cycle deep into her body. She pressed her breasts down onto the sheets, the friction grazing her nipples, tightening them. "Tell me, Gabs, talk to me. Tell me about Adam."

"In the restaurant, Flick, or later?" Gabriela teased her darling, who couldn't keep the springs quiet any more.

"Oh h Gabs. Later? You lucky bitch, fuck. Not fair, I want him too." Felicity would soon knock the phone onto the floor, and faintly hear Gabriela's giggle, then her whisper.

"Come, my darling, make yourself come. I'll stay with you while you do. Naughty Felicity, playing with herself while I talk to you on the phone."

Gabriela told Flick what happened next, her voice low and husky with the memory of it. With her phone on the floor, Gabriela's voice was small and distant. Felicity came, nearly sobbing with her own pleasure, but not quite.

After dinner, where Gabriela had charmed the chef and wondered whether Adam thought the waitress delectable, they drove down to the sea. The low surf was moonlit and phosphorescent, the night sky sprinkled dark with distance. A gentle breeze blew the swirl of Gabriela's dress against her legs and she spun around twice, to show Adam the movement of the skirt. She was luminescent, her long hair midnight black and falling long to her waist.

"The moonlight, Adam, your hair is silver in the moonlight." She took his arm, and they were a couple by the sea, en promenade.

"The flow of your dress, Gabriela, it reminds me of a poem. 'Like a skein of loose silk against a wall.' The woman in the poem is not like you though, she's bored and wants an indiscretion." Adam looked down at the young woman on his arm. "You're not bored."

Gabriela glanced up at him. "No, not at all bored, Adam, not when I'm with you."

"Is this an indiscretion, do you think, you having dinner with me? I'm twice your age. More than." Adam was curious for her response. The confidence revealed in the phone number written in her looping cursive impressed him; but the nervous twisting hands, they intrigued him too. She was two contradictory women, almost, in one lovely package.

"More than twice my age. Yes, you are, but so what?" Gabriela looked straight at him, and her eyes were black, jet black. "All it means is I'm half your age. I don't have a problem with that." She interrogated him. "Do you?"

"No, I don't. Some people might though."

"Oh goodness, who cares? You're not my father, that's the kind of silly thing he worries about." She paused. "Actually, Dad's not so bad. Mum's the nightmare, she's always on at me. 'Gabriela, when are you going to bring a nice young man home?' she'll say. And my answer is always the same. 'I've not met anybody yet, Mum.'" She looked at Adam, thoughtfully. "I wonder what she'd think of you?"

"Gabriela, I'm not a nice young man," Adam replied. "And I'm not sure I'm ready to meet your mother." He laughed. "Is she like you, Gabriela?"

"Stop it. You're teasing. You mustn't. We've only had dinner, and you've taken me to the Japanese Gardens. That's all." She was defending her mother and justifying herself, and knew it wasn't all, not one bit. God, Flick, she thought, I've got three buttons undone on my dress and my sleeves are a lost cause, and I have a velvet choker around my throat; and Adam's talking about my mother. Help, what I do?

"What were you like as a young man, Adam?" She changed the subject, and it was a genuine interest. She tried to picture him at her age, but couldn't. She took his arm again, and leaned her head against his shoulder, steering him back to the car. A cool breeze had sprung up, and she shivered.

"Gabriela, are you getting cold? I shouldn't have brought you here, that was thoughtless of me." Adam placed his arm around her shoulder, draping her with his coat. And it was natural that she placed her arm around his waist and they had a perfect pace together. "There, darling, are you warmer now?"

Gabriela thought of her father, that was exactly the kind of thing he would have said. Would you approve of Adam, Daddy? she thought, and vaguely thought he might. She smiled to herself, and this time Adam didn't see it.

She remembered the boys who courted her at school. "You look after my girl now, she's the only one we've got." Her dad was only half joking when he said it, and the lads were bright enough to know that. "Yes sir, Mr G, I will." Gabriela was always home by eleven, and her dad would pop his head in her door. "How'd it go, Gabs?" Sometimes she would tell him, patting the bed cover for him to sit beside her, her eyes bright with the tell of it. And Gabriela's father learned that his daughter was strong willed with a mind of her own, and unreachable standards all of her own.

"What were you like when you were young?" she repeated. Gabriela was more interested to discover what his young women were like, but didn't know how to lead that question. She thought he might come around to them, his own moments and tells.

"A young man, Gabriela? I don't know if I can remember back that far. It's a long time ago."

"You're not Methuselah or Noah, Adam, even if you do have a biblical name." She wasn't going to let him get away without an answer. "It's not that long ago. You can tell me."

Even in the dark, Adam knew her lashes fluttered up at him and her eyes were innocent and huge. She hugged his arm, to let him know she was playing, and he loved her confidence in teasing him. They were nearly at the car, and he turned to her and placed both hands on her waist. Gabriela wanted to place her hands on his upper arms to feel his strength, but didn't. She left her arms loose by her sides.

"When I was young, Gabriela, someone taught me to do this."

Adam pulled her to him, one hand circling around her waist, the other moving confidently to her back, between her shoulder blades. And he pulled her to him, tilting her head to his. "Taught me this, Gabriela," and he kissed her, long and passionate, holding her close, oh so close.

Gabriela's hands came away from her sides, and one was around his neck, the other on the back of his head, pulling his mouth to hers, pulling him to her, don't let go, don't let go.

She broke the kiss. "Who was she, Adam? What happened?"

"She left me, Gabriela, that's what happened."

My god, thought Gabriela, didn't she know what she was doing, this woman? She reached her hand to his cheek, and felt a tiny weight as Adam rested his head on her palm, like a pillow. Oh, Adam.

"Adam, can we go now? I want to go."

Their moods had changed, like switches suddenly do, and Gabriela wanted him so much. She didn't know what to do, and her heart pounded. Her breasts ached and her nipples were like jewels, hard and firm, and her cunt bloomed. She could picture Adam's head on her shoulder, and that had to be enough, she didn't know any more. *Five buttons, Flick, but I don't know what to do.*

"Sweet Jesus, Gabriela," moaned Flick, her fingers wet within herself, "what did you do?"

The Last Button

Adam took her back to his apartment. It was on the tenth floor of a small high rise, its display windows looking over the parklands, with a distant view to the eastern hills and a glimpse of the bay to the west.

On the way there they were both silent in the car, the shifted mood from the sea and Adam's lost loves hovering over them like ghosts. Gabriela understood this man was carved and bound by the women in his past, and she understood too her innocence ill equipped her for competing with them. She resolved then, that she could only be herself, and that would have to be enough. She could be no more.

Her fingers toyed with the velvet band around her neck, and the movement of her red-tipped fingers was slow. Gabriela was no longer nervous; she walked in the footsteps of his teachers and she did not think he would have known frail and fragile women. Her hand rested on his thigh, a cat's paw quietness, no weight at all.

As they walked from the basement car park to the lift her small hand found his, and they said not a word. Adam knew, even if she did not, her touch was a lifeline. He was still formal with her, ushering her through his door with his hand in the small of her back, then taking her coat from her shoulders like a cloak.

"A drink, Gabriela, what will you have?"

Adam showed her the lounge room, and she stood absorbing the view while he clattered cupboards and clinked glasses in the kitchen.

"Here, my lovely," and Adam stood by her, slightly behind, his tall presence solid in the room. Gabriela rested her head against his shoulder and felt safe. His hand rested gently on Gabriela's waist, just beside the curve of her hip.

Adam placed his glass on a table and moved behind her, his hands cupping the small swell of her belly. Gabriela was astonished by the silent intimacy of this touch, and grateful for his gentleness. She was realising this man was full of care and devotion, so careful towards her, and slow.

The rest of her body was burning with a hot heat, her sex was molten and smouldering for him, and her high breasts hard and tight, her nipples full. Yet this man held her softest swell, her centre, with respectful hands, gentle hands. She didn't know a man could be so gentle.

Or so certain. Adam lifted a hand from Gabriela's belly and slowly unlooped the fourth button on the front of her dress, exposing the full creamy curves of her breasts and the laced tops of her bra cups. Gabriela gasped, and her breasts swelled high. He didn't say a word, but cupped her belly then slid his other hand inside the cut of her dress and cupped a full breast. He trapped her there, in his hands, and even if Gabriela wanted to, she could not have escaped.

She leaned her head back towards his and turned her face up, seeking a kiss. Oh sweet god, Adam, you hold me so close. How do you know what to do?

Oh, my sweet Angel, you turn your lips to mine and your eyes never let me go. Sweet Jesus, is this how love begins? Not again, not now.

"Oh fuck, Gabs, I can't bear it." Felicity clamped her thighs tight on her hand, two fingers deep inside herself in a solitary fuck, her other hand squeezing her breast oh so hard. She ached, but couldn't ease it.

Adam held Gabriela, a full breast in the palm of one hand and the swell of her belly soft in the palm of the other. They were motionless like that for a long moment, then her fingers came up to the fifth silken button on her dress, and she undid it. The undoing revealed both her breasts high, the whole embroidered lace of her bra and its silken cups. Gabriela held the back of Adam's hand and pressed it to her heart.

"Adam, I need to tell you something." It can't wait, not now, not any more.

"Is it important, Gabriela?" He held her close, his hands warm and his body standing firm behind her. "Of course, it must be important, or you wouldn't be telling me."

He let her go, and turned her towards him, smoothly pulling the sides of her dress together so she was unrevealed. Gabriela held the unbuttoned dress together with one hand, pulling it up close to her throat. She held his gaze. He held both his hands to her waist and looked upon her. She placed her hand on one of his, taking confidence from the touch of him.

"I... you're my first, Adam, you'll be my first man." She didn't look away. "If you continue to undress me, that is." Undress me, Adam, I want you to.

Adam's hands remained motionless about her, and the moment turned in on itself.

Her heart beat faster and she took another breath, a double intake that was almost a sob, but not quite.

"I..." Adam stopped. Ahh, I see. Me? "You've never... Me, you want me to be the first man you sleep with?"

"Yes. No. I don't know. Yes."

Gabriela, normally so sure of herself, was no longer sure at all. Could she trust this man, trust him fully and deeply enough to give him her greatest gift? Between her legs her cunt opened and bloomed and wetness slipped, and she ached to give him herself. The gift of her trust, her complete and unconditional trust. To feel a man within herself, finally, fully and completely and hers, all hers.

Gabriela wanted this. Her cunt wettened and the base of her belly tightened, and a long ache began. Gabriela's fingers turned and were nervous at her wrist, playing with the cuff on her sleeve. She held the folds of her dress together, hiding her breasts as she revealed her truth.

Adam gazed at her, his mind shifting quickly through the imponderables of her request, at the enormity of her gift, the responsibility.

"Why me?" She had reduced him to fundamental questions.

"Why you? Why you, Adam? Don't you know?" Gabriela looked at him, more certain now. "It's you, Adam, because I trust you. You'll never let me fall. You're too kind for that." She held his eyes, refusing to let her gaze drop, and reached her hand up to his cheek.

Adam tilted his head to rest it against the tiny pillow of her palm and could sleep there.

"Silly boys and young men, Adam, they could never catch me if I fell." Gabriela believed in him. "You'll always keep me safe."

Adam lifted his hands from her waist to her face, and cradled her cheeks like a prayer. He held her for a moment then fell into the blackness of her eyes. She closed her eyes, trapping the vision of him in her mind, and now her world was touch. Gabriela gave herself up to him completely, and didn't need light to see.

Adam gently took her hand from her throat, and she let go of the cloth. Her hands dropped by her sides, and she stood before him.

Slowly, and without a word, Adam undid the remaining three buttons of her dress, three silken buttons and they were all undone. He took one step back from her, and slid the dress back from her shoulders. It fell to the floor with the softest sigh of silk, and she stood before him, her head high, proud. Her eyes were closed, but she knew Adam gazed upon her, his eyes revelling in her revelation.

Gabriela stood before him in simple lingerie, delicate and tasteful, soft against her skin, lightly embroidered. The garments were a paleness against her tanned skin, hiding and revealing every curve. Black stockings on her legs, black straps to a plain garter around her waist.

"Your shoes, you don't need them anymore." Adam's voice was low.

Gabriela stepped from her heels, and they fell inside the puddle of her dress. She stood delicate before him, her hands by her sides, her long hair falling.

"Gabriela, you're beautiful. Let me look at you."

She let him see, but kept her own eyes closed. Too much.

"Wait." Gabriela heard a quiet slide of fingers on cloth, and felt the movement of air and a drop of cloth. She guessed Adam had pulled his shirt from his body and dropped it to the floor. She stood before him, still.

And felt him close. With a deft touch, Adam reached behind Gabriela and took the strap of her bra between his fingers, unclipping it from her back. She felt the whimsy cloth drop away, the straps sliding from her shoulders, and the weight of her breasts were heavy on her chest. They were pressed against him, her hot flesh against the heat of him.

Adam's hands curved around her back, and he held her naked torso to his. Gabriela placed her hands softly against his back, and if he was an angel, would have felt wings. She nuzzled her lips to the base of his throat, tasting his skin. Adam's hands lifted through the silken smoothness of her hair and he cradled the back of her head.

"Gabriela," he whispered, "it's me, I'm here."

"You are, Adam, here with me." They were simple vows, and the truth of the moment.

For Gabriela, seconds ticked by and the moment grew longer and longer and it was all there was, everything forever. Her heart beat was uncounted, always ever.

Adam's time spiralled in on itself and his time stopped, nothing, no more, never. He needed to hear Gabriela's heart, to be alive.

"Wait," he said, "just a moment."

Gabriela opened her eyes to see him go from the room, his naked back and broad shoulders. She knew his shape from his suits in the morning, and liked what she saw. She looked down upon herself and saw her full breasts, tipped hard with dark nipples, darker brown against her dark skin, and liked what she saw. Gabriela covered both breasts with her arms, suddenly shy, not yet used to nakedness with anybody but Felicity.

Adam must have known, for he returned with a long embroidered gown and draped it around her back, hiding her luscious curves. The cool cloth felt wonderful on her skin, soft and smooth.

"Thank you, Adam. It's a beautiful gown." She turned on her toes, a small pirouette to show him and to hide herself.

"Japanese, it's late nineteenth century. But I'm not sure where from, or who would have worn it, back then."

Gabriela wrapped herself in it and was coy. But coyness was no match for Adam's confidence, for he simply knelt before her, split the drape of the gown from Gabriela's thighs and unclipped the garter straps from the tops of her stockings. He then peeled the knickers from her hips and slipped them down her legs. Still kneeling, he pressed his cheek to her small swelling belly, and held himself there, one arm stretched up her back, under the cloth of the gown.

The triangle of dark hair was soft to the touch of his palm as he cupped the mound of her Venus, his fingers splayed upwards to her navel. Gabriela still stood with her legs together, but she could feel the heat of her cunt blaze within her.

Adam stood, and wrapped the gown around her. "Don't get cold," he said. "Stay warm." I can wait, he thought, she'll open the gown when she's ready.

I'm not quite ready yet, thought Gabriela. But how can I still be dressed when he's just undressed me? How many veils will he strip from my skin before he sees me?

"Come, Gabriela, come through to my room."

"Fuuck," keened Flick, as Gabriela told her the tell. "Fuck, Gabs, will you tell me what happened? Don't you bloody dare hang up. You've got me dripping here, listen." And she held the phone down near her sex and Gabriela could hear the slick and wet slide of Flick's fingers.

"But Flick, he's barely touched me at this stage." Gabriela teased her friend, and was wet herself as she remembered.

Adam pulled back the covers on his bed, and split wide the curtains so moonlight poured into the room. The apartment was on the tenth floor, impossible to overlook, high above the streets so nobody else mattered and the world was far away.

Gabriela watched as Adam disappeared into the bathroom where she heard a run of water and some quiet movement. Despite her inevitable countdown towards moments she could only imagine, Gabriela was calm within herself. Her pulse was fast but steady, and with her cuffs gone and silken buttons undone, there was nothing left to hold onto in twists and turns. So she settled like a cat settles, curled and calm.

She heard the light switch click, and she looked up as Adam came into the room naked, walked to the window and stood there. He said nothing and let Gabriela see him. She looked, and saw the silvery gray hair on his head, his long limbs still slender, and his ass not quite so tight as once it might have been, but still shapely.

"Turn around, Adam, I want to see you walk towards me."

He did so, and Gabriela saw fine silvery hair on his chest, going darker down onto his gut. She saw the thick hang of his cock long against his thigh and liked the shape of him. Adam was full but not hard, the head of his cock still partly covered by his foreskin. A line of darker hair ran from his navel down around the base of his cock and over the swell of his balls. As he walked towards the bed, his cock swung and began to thicken at the promise of her.

"Adam, come to me." Gabriela held her arms out wide to him, inviting him to her body and would cradle his head to her heart. Her nipples were thick and hard, and her sex wet, so wet.

She turned ever so slightly on the bed with one arm outstretched on the sheet, and Adam lay beside her, his body covering half of hers. He kissed her with the softest kiss and tasted her lips, then ran his mouth, a warm breath, down the side of her throat. Adam lay his head on her shoulder and heard her heartbeat and was held by her.

He had all the time in the night with Gabriela, and over his years he had learned slowness and patience. Adam thought she would give herself to him in her own time and in her own way, and he wondered what moods might wash over her as her arousal heightened. He knew from her stories of Felicity that Gabriela knew her pleasure and how to find it, but now she would be discovering a man, learning his pleasure too, and how to share it. Ah woman, he thought, we will be wonderful together.

"Gabriela," he whispered, just to hear her name.

"What is it, Adam?" Her voice was low. She rested her hand on his shoulder and his skin was surprisingly soft.

"Oh, I just like the sound of your name. Gabriela." He looked up to her face and touched her cheek with his fingers, lightly, a delicate touch.

She smiled down at him, her eyes bright and alive. She took his fingers in hers and touched them to her lips. "Gabriela," she said her own name for him and it was her second gift.

They lay still for a minute or two, no longer caring about time for there was plenty of it. Adam began a slow, languid discovery of Gabriela's body, lingering his fingers over the curve of her shoulder, down into the long scoop of her waist, curving his palm over the swell of her hips and over her ass. His movements were slow, his hands stopping every now and then to caress another curve. Gabriela's skin prickled with goose bumps and he made his slow circuits a little heavier, shivering sensation into her.

Gabriela moaned with the pleasure of him, low in her throat, and her fingers began a different caress, more tentative, exploratory. She found sensitive places just inside his hip where her touch made him shiver, and she remembered them, learning Adam's delicate places. They shifted together on the bed, and Gabriela's legs slowly parted and his fingers found her.

Their hands continued curious wanderings, and slowly they rearranged themselves on the bed. Adam's cheek rested on her thigh, his face inches from her sex, glistening beads of wetness on her lips shimmering under the silvering moonlight.

Oh sweet goodness, Adam slid his fingers into her, and her hands stopped still. He tasted her, and offered up his fingers to her mouth so she could taste herself.

Gabriela's lick of his fingers was wet and warm, and she sucked the fingers into her mouth and made them hot and slick with her own saliva. She slid her own fingers into her cunt dark place, exposing the nub of her clit to his eyes, showing Adam how she stroked herself, sliding two fingers around the thickness of her clitoris.

Shimmering, shuddering, she touched herself and Adam gazed on her, concentrating on her fingers in herself, learning how she slid fast and circled slow. Her leg twitched, and he pressed his hand onto the back of hers and made her slow and stop.

"There's so much time, Gabriela, don't rush."

"I want all of you now, Adam, I'm greedy for you." Gabriela took her cunt wet fingers from her centre and, finding his long shaft by her face, slid a shining line with her finger along the length of him, and over the head of his cock. Fascinated, she chased after the shaft as it bounced from her touch, curling her fingers around it to hold him still. "Adam, your cock, it's so hot, feel the heat of you." She was amazed, finding for the first time so much heat.

Gabriela slid the circle of her fingers down the shaft, and over the head of it. "So soft, the head. Adam, it's incredible. I didn't know a man's skin could be so soft."

Adam closed his eyes with the pleasure of her slow discovery of his cock, and denied himself the wonder in her eyes as she touched him.

Gabriela was tentative with her touch, so delicate. She didn't yet know that she could grip him hard as well as stroke him soft. She curved the palm of her hand over the end of his cock, and he shuddered with the near pain of it. Gabriela saw his reaction, and stilled her grip, two hands now.

"Don't stop, ahh, that's good."

Gabriela tightened her hold on his shaft, and stroked slowly, firmer movements now, and was rewarded by a throb of his cock. "Oh, I see," she whispered, and touched Adam like she touched her own clitoris. "It's like me, only thicker and long." She measured the length of him with her thumb and fingers spread wide, and her hand was too small to know all his length.

She pressed her palm against Adam's side. "On your back," her low voice a command but he wouldn't say no. She rearranged herself on the bed, with her head resting on Adam's chest for a pillow, facing his cock which was the centre of her study now. She needed to know the length of him, his thickness that would be hers, the colour but he was silver in the moonlight, the softness of his skin which was hot velvet and smooth. Gabriela learned the cooler fragile weight of Adam's balls and they were big in the cup of her hands.

She tasted the length of his shaft with her tongue, and she kissed his cock sideways and left a kiss of her lipstick on him that was black in the moonlight, red in the morning when the sun rose; but the birds were asleep and there would be a cleansing place soon.

Adam coiled her long hair in his hand and breathed in its smell and felt its softness on his face, and he was filled with the sensation of her, this young woman discovering him in her new way. "Gabriela," he whispered, and she paused to hear his words but only heard his silence and his faster breath.

"I'm Gabriela," she whispered back, an affirmation of who she was and why she was here. She moved a little, opening her mouth around him for the first time, and took the plum of his cock head onto her tongue.

Gabriela slowed, to remember the stretch of her lips and the heat, the hard heat in her mouth. Her saliva flowed and the heat rose. Gabriela sucked on his head and made him moan. She did it again, and he moaned again. His hand gripped her hair and his body twitched.

Gabriela smiled to herself and released him. "There's so much time, Adam, don't rush." She trapped him once more, and her hands were slow on his shaft and her tongue twisted and curled.

Adam began a long stroke of Gabriela's back, down into the tight valley of her waist and over her rounded ass, along her thighs, turning his hand back up her spine. He found the long tightness between her thighs, and with each long sweep of his hand he teased fingers between her legs and she opened to him wider, until again his fingers found her wet centre and her musky scent, stronger now, was dusk and darkness in the air.

My turn, he thought, to taste her deep into my mouth, to drink her juice. "On your back, Gabriela, it's your turn."

She released his cock and obeyed, would never not. Her eyes were wide to the wonder of him, and they kissed but Adam was gone and her legs fell wide and her eyes closed. Adam knelt on the floor beside the bed, and took her thighs up in his arms, spreading her wide. She opened to him and wanted it all.

Adam placed the warm palm of his hand over Gabriela's sex, cupping the centre of her wet heat. With his other hand he reached up her body and felt the weight of a breast, rolling a hard nipple between his finger and thumb. For a long moment he held her sexual centres, joining them together through his own body and channelling his own energy around her.

He lifted his hand from her sex, and covered her with his open mouth, tasting her honeyed sweetness with his lips. Gabriela gasped at the heat from his mouth. Her hand pressed his to her breast. Adam probed the wet lips with his tongue and it was a little fuck. He swirled his tongue up and around her clit, licking her risen nub, sucking her hot centre into his mouth. Gabriela bucked up against his mouth, and was eaten by him. "Ahhh, more," she sighed, "yes."

Adam licked and probed, alternating between circles around her clit, then a firm tongue over the head of it, then descending to lose himself in the depths of her cunt. Gabriela moaned for him, "Mmmm, oh yes, there," and he settled to the perfect rhythm, pulling her sex to his mouth until it was all there was, a hot mouthing fuck into her. Slowly he licked Gabriela up to a first throbbing peak, then released her and did it again, surging sensation into her heat, her aching sex, and she came. Pushing her body down onto his mouth, Gabriela came, and a minute later came again.

Adam's ebb and flow against her cunt was relentless, until she came once more and pushed his face away from her sex. "Stop, it's too much." Gabriela cupped her own hand over her centre, pressing and pressing as she descended from the height of her pleasure, falling away from the strength of him and his control over her. "Oh sweet man, my god, look what you do to me."

Gabriela lay sprawled on the bed, her legs spread wide and her sex lips were dark and swollen, her juice glistening in the moonlight. Adam stood up from the floor and lowered his weight onto her, his long cock a burning heat on the flesh of her belly. Adam kissed the taste of her onto her mouth, and she sucked on his ripe lips, tasting herself and mingling his taste.

Gabriela wrapped her arms around his back, not letting him go, pulling his weight down onto her breasts, holding him, holding him. "I'm not letting you go, Adam, you sweet man. How do you know?"

"How do I know what, Gabriela?"

"How to make me helpless, a wreck." She kissed him, hard. "More."

"Gabs, I'm dripping here. I'm so wet my sheets are wet, sweet Jesus."

"Oh Flick, maybe I'd better end the call, so's you can get some sleep." Gabriela teased her friend, knowing the last thing she wanted was sleep, and knowing the first thing Felicity wanted was Adam, or a man like Adam.

"Don't you bloody dare hang up." Flick was in agony and ecstasy listening to Gabs tell of her seduction and sex, sultry and slow.

"More."

.

Adam gave Gabriela more. He had no choice, he was enraptured by this virgin woman, trapped by her, spellbound. He was no longer Merlin unbound, he was seduced, bound by her, trapped in her tree.

Adam lifted his weight from Gabriela and slowly moved back down over her body, his lips butterfly kisses on her neck and down over the small curve of her shoulder. He took her hand in his and reminded Gabriela where each of her silken buttons were.

"Two on each wrist, Gabriela, and the first ones undone in a Japanese garden." He kissed her wrist and saw a tiny pulse beat there, the smallest heart under her skin.

"Yes, and another two there. I was so daring, wasn't I?" She smiled at her memory, and the fall of leaves in a garden would forever remind her of him, and his silence there.

"Wicked, Gabriela, so bad."

"And Ruth's buttons, making me a temptress, show me where they were, Adam."

"Here." At the base of her neck, a kiss, just below the black velvet choker which was the last garment of her nudity for him.

"And here." Another kiss, on the slope of her chest, where the blaze of her freckles began. Gabriela's skin shivered, and her nipples tightened.

"And here, Gabriela," and he touched his lips to the crease of her cleavage where the spray of sun kissed freckles ended. Her sex bloomed, and where she was wet before, Gabriela wettened once more, her whole belly an empty ache, full of longing.

Adam suckled her tight nipples, one at a time, and Gabriela offered each breast up to him in her hands, then soothed the tightness with her hands pressed hard.

"The last buttons, Adam," Gabriela whispered, "before my dress dropped away. Where were they?"

Adam didn't speak, but showed her, trailing his tongue down the centre of her body towards her navel. He kissed her there, and her belly rose with an intake of breath, a gasping sigh. He kissed her again, where the finest thread of darkness furred a tiny seam on her skin, a dark trail moving down.

"Then what did you do Adam?" Gabriela's voice was the softest whisper, almost to herself, as she remembered her moments forever. "Oh god, yes."

Again, Adam took her sex into his mouth, his hot heat surrounding her sex, and their lips joined in a kiss, her sex lips swollen and dark. Adam tasted her, she was liquorice and honey with a delicate tang.

Adam made sure she was wet, so wet, then placed himself between her legs. Taking his cock in his hand, he carefully placed the head of it between her sex lips and held himself there, waiting for Gabriela to be ready.

Adam held his weight above her, gazed into the blackness of her eyes, and began to fall.

Gabriela knew exactly where he was, this man who waited for her, and she lay still beneath him. Still, so still, and she felt her heartbeat pulsing deep within her.

"Yes," she whispered to herself, and gave herself to him, this man she had waited for.

Adam gave himself up to her. As he slid slowly into her tightness, so slowly, Gabriela undid the clasp of the choker around her neck, so when she reached to his mouth for a kiss, a welcoming kiss, the velvet band fell from her throat and she was free and naked for him.

As he sank his length into Gabriela's sex, she struggled to keep her eyes open, gazing up into his. Adam paused, holding himself still within her, and Gabriela's eyes widened. Finally, as another inch slid inside her and she began to shudder with the pleasure of their joining, her eyes closed. Her throat and chest were flushed a deep red and Adam sank further, slow small thrusts, until his whole length was in her, flesh against flesh, heat within heat.

Gabriela whimpered, small wordless sounds in her throat, ohh, ohh, and she had him deep inside her body. Yes, mine, she thought and took him in. Adam felt huge inside her, and her whole sensation shifted to her cunt, her clit. Adam moved within her. Gabriela opened her legs wider, raising her thighs to his hips, taken, utterly taken.

Oh sweet love, Adam moved within her, long thrusts and slow. With the greatest care, with the greatest tenderness, he placed his arms under her knees and pushed them back with her thighs wide and high. Gabriela was spread, open, taking him in, and trusting Adam implicitly to love her love her love her as he slid his beautiful cock into her in slow, delicious thrusts.

Ohh, she sighed. Adam was so gentle, too gentle, her heart ached with his softness as he shafted her with his long cock, finally piercing the aching dam that had been building up all evening, all the long days, a deep swelling flow of heat and spreading sensation from deep inside her belly.

Gabriela opened herself for him, and he was in her, deep, one arm wrapped under her neck now, cradling her head to his, her cheek against his cheek, his lips soft kisses on hers. Oh yes, she sighed, love me, fuck me, my beautiful man, take me, take me. Make me yours.

She opened her eyes and held his gaze as he shafted into her, long and thick into the depths of her body, heat and sweat and a faster movement now, her pleasure a hot keen of ecstasy as she peaked in colours and white light, her body throbbing and shuddering under him as she came, her first orgasm with a cock inside her.

And her second, moments later, a long slow moment, wet and hard, pulsating around him. Gabriela thrust up to meet Adam, clenching his thick long shaft, rhythmic squeezes of her cunt like a hand. Gabriela's mouth was hungry for his, sucking in his tongue, eating his lips, fucking her tongue up into his mouth as he fucked her deep open cunt, faster now and Gabriela was helpless, helpless as he surged into her.

Adam felt a long deep heat at the base of his spine as his cum thickened and surged until with long thrusts, two and three pumps, his cum jetted hard as his back arched above her, creaming cum pulsed into Gabriela. The spill peaked her once more, "Yes," she cried, "oh h, ye es!" Her cries rang out in the room, a sudden scream silenced.

"I'm coming," Adam echoed her cry, "ahh h," and they surged and fucked and came together, high heat and white light and their eyes seeing nothing, and they came, clutching and holding and never letting go, they came together.

Gabriela clung to him and pulled his weight down onto her body, feeling his solidity covering her fragility. She shuddered with aftershocks rippling through her, long waves of pleasure taking her breath, gasping breaths nearly sobs but laughing too. Her glow began, that long warm place where heat became warmth, swift movements turned to slow caresses, and she fell silent.

Still inside her, Adam rolled on to his side and wrapped his arms around Gabriela, and hugged her to his chest. Safe, so safe. She smiled up at him and touched his cheek and he was there. Hers, this man, this lovely man.

They murmured to each other, low whispers and soft laughter, as they descended from the soaring heights of their orgasms. Their fingers traced spirals and patterns on each other's skin, and they became still in the night. At some point Adam shifted and his softened cock eased from her. Gabriela rolled away from him, their juice left a shining trail on her hip.

She nestled her ass back against Adam's groin and felt his heat there. She smiled, marvelling at the softness where once there had been hardness. Gabriela drifted into sleep, Adam's hand warm on her belly, cupping the small mound of it. Later, he too slept, and she was warm and small as he spooned her.

Several hours later Gabriela stirred, a chill on her skin from the cooler night air. "Pull the covers up, Daddy, I'm cold," she whispered, still asleep, not knowing where she was, who she was with.

In the morning Gabriela woke first. She crept from the bed and went to the bathroom. After she flushed, she looked at herself in the mirror, carefully, tilting her head first one way then the other. I'm no different, she thought, not really. She contemplated herself once more, looking at herself in the mirror, quite still, a serious look on her face.

She decided. Gabriela put her hair up in a twisted coil, and snapped a band about it. She took every ring off from her fingers, her studs and diamonds from her ears, and gazed upon herself, utterly naked.

Proudly, Gabriela walked back to the bedroom. She went to the bed, pulled back the covers, and lay her head on Adam's chest. She gently placed a hand on his soft, sleeping cock and held it there, not moving.

In time, Adam grew hard and Gabriela held him, still not moving. When he finally stirred, waking slowly, she let his shaft go. She rolled on to her front, then kneeled, raising her lush ass high and placing her weight on her elbows. Gabriela's full breasts swung below her body, and she presented herself for Adam's morning pleasure. She took him very deep into her body - he was already deep in her soul.

"I don't get it, Gabs," pondered Felicity later that week. "Why did you take off the choker and all of your jewellery?"

"Because I wanted to be utterly naked for him, totally exposed and open for him; me, unadorned." Gabriela paused. "I trust him absolutely, Flick, but he doesn't own me." She took the long blackness of her hair in one hand and let it fall over her forearm and her fingers.

"I'll go to him again, of course I will." She remembered every-thing. "How could I not?"

She wanted him and she'd give herself, gladly, as a gift, but he held no claim over her, none at all.

About the Author

A.A. Cain is an author of erotic tales living somewhere in suburban Australia. His work has been described as, "almost poetic; stories told by a crackling fire on a cold winter night, with a smooth whiskey in hand, listeners curled at your feet."

Cain's stories move from the floating world of city cafés and fashionable galleries, with contemp- orary men and women finding pleasure in familiar places, through to mysterious, mythical worlds populated with angels and astronauts, mermaids and men, and always, dark, seductive women.

Readers' Comments

"Intoxicatingly slow."

"So erotic and wonderfully sensual."

"Much as I love many of the stories on here... this must be my all time favourite. So tender... so erotic... so sensual... thank you so much for allowing me to enjoy."

"Oh my! What an incredible talent you have with 26 letters, turning them into words and paragraphs and forming incredibly sharp images in my mind. Wonderful storytelling, taking me away in my old age to another sweet time when that first blush of love consumes us. Thank you, dear writer."

"Wonderfully executed... a trip to another time and place."

"What a beautiful read. I felt it in my toes. Only way it could be any sexier is if someone read it to me... Mmmm."

"I don't know how many times I have read this story, but I keep coming back and reading it again as it so incredibly beautifully written."
"This was an intense sexual pleasurable read, thanks so much I deeply enjoyed."

"I liked part two very much. I adore stories that include men with men. Men like to read about, and watch, women together, don't they? I like to read about, and watch, men together. I can tell from your writing how much you love women - the way they look and taste and smell and walk and sit and kiss. I feel like that about some men - and some women."

"Wow! Wonderful. Like a long ski run or a running river, sometimes in control and sometimes not. An opportunity to have control, relinquish control and savor both. Satisfaction."

"I've read a lot of erotica - I write it too - and you have blown me away. (Pun intended.) I love the patience, the slowness, how you focus on every single sense when you're describing a scene."

"You've made this woman very happy tonight:"

"I admire that amazingly languid style that you have. You manage to draw these moments out for sentence after sentence, but I never get impatient with it. While reading some authors is like waiting on queue at the DMV, reading you is more like lounging in a bath on a Sunday afternoon. I don't entirely understand how you do it. Your prose and your dialog are very formal and elegant. That usually drives me nuts, but somehow, the way you do it, it just flows so beautifully."

"I have not seen a parallel of true erotic storytelling. The ability to build so slowly to a climax. To describe feelings and sensations not just a description of physical movements."

Comments by Jaimie Stone:

I can see why your female readers like you. Amanda is a very likable love interest. You treat her with respect. She's a working woman. She's not objectified until... until she's ready for it, is what I want to say? When she notices Adam's attention on her, and begins to angle for more? Adam is patient, and attentive, and very very likeable. He's confident but also willing to simply give a foot massage a propos of nothing, and if that doesn't win you some romance readers nothing will.

I had to really look for that, though. The characterization was almost lost among the driftwood, because the story doesn't... do anything. RamosWashington's Bootcamp for Boyfriends had the abstract of "Yankee city boy goes south and meets a Southern Belle, and she turns him into a man." Comforting my Sister's abstract would be something like "Broken hearted young girl with small tits gets dumped because she has small tits, and turns to the only person who doesn't seem to care that she has small tits; her brother."

The abstract for The Floating World would be like… "Man meets many people in the course of his day to day life?" In the big picture sense, there isn't a plot. Adam goes here and has some coffee and we start to meet a woman that he has a connection with, but that ends fairly abruptly. It seems like you were setting that up to be some kind of deep existential crisis for Adam, but then you skipped to someplace else where he very quickly struck up a similar sort of unspoken connection with a Middle Eastern woman (cudos for giving her some body hair).

In your opening, you describe that the title is derived from a Japanese phrase that means "Meaningless pleasure". You took that concept and made something interesting out of it, but meaningless is a pretty terrible place to try and start building erotica. It's like building your castle in a swamp. Even if you execute every possible angle, you're starting off in a bad place and that's going to limit the overall potential.

It's nearly one full Lit page before we meet Amanda, and it's not even clear that she's going to be any more important than the previous two baristas until maybe the middle of the second Lit page. Now, I'm all for a long drawn-out build up, but making the reader guess who will be important later on "feels" like even you didn't know where you would end up when you started. Meandering down different streets and sometimes finding dead ends. Even if that's not true, it's how it "feels".

To me, this is a two-fold problem. One is the large-scale plotting, and the second is pacing. I was fully on board with the story of Adam and his slow relationship with the first barista. Fool me once. I was skeptical with the Middle Eastern woman. I was straight up disbelieving of Amanda. Even once you establish Amanda as the love interest, there's a lot of walking around. Going here and there. A lot of dodging glances and the internal gymnastics of "What did THAT look mean?!" The places they go don't matter to the plot. They don't serve a purpose. It's like looking at someone else's GPS history.

These two aspects, plotting and pacing, really come together to make a weird problem where your scenes run together without any kind of divide. It's difficult to sort out what is happening and when in relation to the other thing that just happened.

Stories should have peaks and valleys of tension. In a romance, your peaks of tension should be visceral moments where the POV is right in the middle of the action, following an exhilarating and interesting conversation between two intelligent people, and then your valley would be the introspective moments after when the POV character thinks back and says "Wow. What a woman." There's no delineation between these things in The Floating World. Conversations on consecutive days run into each other, and it's hard to feel like I, as the reader, am supposed to be immediately present with Adam for a 24 hour period that you skip in a single paragraph.

You need scene breaks. Break your scenes up, and take care to give them proper beginning and endings. Each scene should be a small vignette within the larger story. The first half of the story, especially before Amanda really shows up, is a muddy swamp of overlapping and concatenated scenes.

Plotting has several layers to it. I feel like The Floating World struggled with the large-scale plotting, but at a scene level it was better. Slow and langorous, yes, but better; especially so in the second half of the story. Although I felt like the places the characters decided to go were haphazard, once they got there they were good together. The characters interacted well. In the TV and movie world, it's called Blocking. How characters move through a dynamic room, full of other characters. The little touches that flesh out the world. The way Amanda having been on her feet all day at work kept coming back around.

The confidence that Adam has, that I mentioned earlier? That's your confidence, and it shows up best in this aspect. You control the later scenes really well, especially in the second half of the story.

The sex scene largely had me feeling left out. It was well written, but the characters developed some very intimate pet names for each other very quickly, and while I have no problem with characters bonding I didn't understand why it was happening in this particular instance. Maybe it has something to do with the way I'm very reserved in real life, and only share that kind of intimacy after a lengthy "getting to know you" period. In The Floating World, that intimacy feels unjustified, and thus feels either forced or fake.

Mostly, what I felt was that the story needed some kind of driving impetus. Something that gives some color to his motivation. As it is, it feels like we're just watching Adam on a regular Tuesday where he maybe kind of bumps into his soulmate and immediately begins addressing her as such. Even if you cut out the false starts in chemistry with the first two baristas (and I think you should), the stuff with Amanda is largely aimless. Drifting.

Author's Reply:

May I say, a brilliant critique, and may I also say I have no issues with what you write. You "got" it entirely - your word is "drifting", my word is "floating".

That's the point, there IS no point. In the words of Pete Townshend (songwriter for The Who), Adam is "living a life of sweet ennui". He is aimlessly wandering through his streets, his life, nothing happening, watching, and waiting. Drifting in his existential angst, perhaps.

There's no real plot. It's an encounter. It's not linear, not really going anywhere. It's got the logic of a dream - linear in the scene, jump, linear in the next scene, shift.

Anti story? I don't know. A mood-piece? Yes, and I think that's why I received the comments I have for this story - my readers (a mix of men and women, I think) were responding to mood, and perhaps the still places I write about, the quiet contemplation.

Thank you again for reading this so closely and taking the time to compose your own words in response.

Flowers and Willows by Hector Bidon (a pseudonym):

OK. Floating world, drifting world. But the story is as much Amanda's as it is Adam's, and hers is the "flower and willow world." To say that nothing happens kind of misses the point. The willow shimmers, the flower blooms. We contemplate their beauty, we inhale their gentle fragrance.

Besides, it's not clear to me that Adam really is plagued by the ennui that claims to be the necessary backdrop of the floating world. We do not really get to see him outside the coffee shops until his excursion with Amanda (at least in this chapter, which is all I've read so far). Perhaps he is happily married and has an important job that unfortunately requires frequent travel.

Or let me put it this way. Who of us in our happily married, importantly employed lives, does not interact with pretty baristas, perky supermarket check-out girls, warm-hearted, ever-smiling Hunan restaurant proprietresses. And who among us has not wondered, at least in passing, whether, despite the differences in age and social standing, she might not really be the one. And suppose that we had been away on a business trip, and suppose that we had encountered her heading in our direction, and suppose that our pleasantries had turned to pleasant flirtation, and suppose that she had been open to coming along to the exhibition, and suppose . . . So a fantasy, sure, but not necessarily a floating one. One that could well be grounded in our own everyday life.

Anyway, regardless of the big picture, the story itself---their romantic encounter---is engaging and delightful. They've already established a chemistry from Adam's visits to the coffee shop. Did he engineer bumping into her that afternoon? I'd like to think not, that it was just serendipitous. The way that the afternoon developed, at least, was spontaneous and mutual. The familiar, teasing banter, the more direct flirtation. "Are you in a hurry to get home?" "No, not really. Why?" He so sincerely delighted by her youth and her vibrancy, she so sincerely delighted by his confidence and his attention. Step by step they improvise their dance.

I've always been partial to first person narration for conveying the intimate details of a character's inner life. But this story wonderfully shows how third person narration can be used to convey the inner activity of two characters, even during the intricate steps of their dance. We see the evening not as we would see it in real life---where we know our own feelings but can only guess at our partner's---but privy to both sides, able to see the uncertainty and hopefulness and playfulness and arousal on both sides as flirtation turns to courtship and courtship turns to foreplay. It's two intimate stories, really, interwoven at every scene. A tour-de-force of patient, loving, doubly imagined detail.

Elegant Seduction of a "Nipponaphile" by 1Penny4My2Cents

Rich in sensuality and the raw sexuality of the *shunga* or *makura-e* (erotic artwork of old) alluded to, but I saw this as more, much more! For me, this trilogy formed a work of art like a painting on a three panel Asian screen; light, shadow, texture, and folds make each separate section beautiful on its own, expanded and viewed in whole its beauty grows almost overwhelming.

Filled with brushstroke tributes to Japan, her history, culture, and people, upon a background of silk, woven from your descriptions like the finest strands, running throughout: of ladies hair, the skein of a poems quote, hosiery, a velvet collar, "just a dress" vintage and pale blue, another cream with twelve buttons, and elegant aged kimonos all softly rustling like the whisper of Maiko walking back alleys of Gion, each piece a fleeting glimpse in a museum tour of "haute couture".

The attention to details when describing the lovely barristas preparing latte in early morning cafés drawn as a parallel to the same slowing of time and separateness of movement observed by the geisha in pouring sake with ceremony in late night teahouses; each simple motion humble, sacred, seductive, loving.

While sharing bits of "the story within" of each character, you continue unfolding the screen, unrolling the storyline before us (perhaps more to come, one can hope!), as you select words, writing with the same deceptive simplicity, grace, and skill that an accomplished calligrapher shows with each stroke, letter, word, line, and scroll a work of art, as petals form buds, blooms, and blossoms, the Sakura... With a low bow I whisper *arigato gozaimashita* for the pleasure of reading this story!